Christmas Stories

Shirt Stories by Lucy Maude Montgomery

Compiled 2016 by
Figgy Tree Publishers

Lucy Maud Montgomery was born at Clifton (now New London), Prince Edward Island, Canada, on November 30, 1874. She achieved international fame in her lifetime, putting Prince Edward Island and Canada on the world literary map. Best known for her "Anne of Green Gables" books, she was also a prolific writer of short stories and poetry. She published some 500 short stories and poems and twenty novels before her death in 1942.

*　　*　　*　　*　　*

A Christmas Inspiration

"Well, I really think Santa Claus has been very good to us all," said Jean Lawrence, pulling the pins out of her heavy coil of fair hair and letting it ripple over her shoulders.

"So do I," said Nellie Preston as well as she could with a mouthful of chocolates. "Those blessed home folks of mine seem to have divined by instinct the very things I most wanted."

It was the dusk of Christmas Eve and they were all in Jean Lawrence's room at No. 16 Chestnut Terrace. No. 16 was a boarding-house, and boarding-houses are not proverbially cheerful places in which to spend Christmas, but Jean's room, at least, was a pleasant spot, and all the girls had brought their Christmas presents in to show each other. Christmas came on Sunday that year and the Saturday evening mail at Chestnut Terrace had been an exciting one.

Jean had lighted the pink-globed lamp on her table and the mellow light fell over merry faces as the girls chatted about their gifts. On the table was a big white box heaped with roses that betokened a bit of Christmas extravagance on somebody's part. Jean's brother had sent them to her from Montreal, and all the girls were enjoying them in common.

No. 16 Chestnut Terrace was overrun with girls generally. But just now only five were left; all the others had gone home for Christmas, but these five could not go and were bent on making the best of it.

Belle and Olive Reynolds, who were sitting on the bed--Jean could never keep them off it--were High School girls; they were said to be always laughing, and even the fact that they could not go home for Christmas because a young brother had measles did not dampen their spirits.

Beth Hamilton, who was hovering over the roses, and Nellie Preston, who was eating candy, were art students, and their homes were too far away to visit. As for Jean Lawrence, she was an orphan, and had no home of her own. She worked on the staff of one of the big city newspapers and the other girls were a little in awe of her cleverness, but her nature was a "chummy" one and her room was a favourite rendezvous. Everybody liked frank, open-handed and hearted Jean.

"It was so funny to see the postman when he came this evening," said Olive. "He just bulged with parcels. They were sticking out in every direction."

"We all got our share of them," said Jean with a sigh of content.
"Even the cook got six--I counted."
"Miss Allen didn't get a thing--not even a letter," said Beth quickly.
Beth had a trick of seeing things that other girls didn't.

"I forgot Miss Allen. No, I don't believe she did," answered Jean thoughtfully as she twisted up her pretty hair. "How dismal it must be to be so forlorn as that on Christmas Eve of all times. Ugh! I'm glad I have friends."

"I saw Miss Allen watching us as we opened our parcels and letters,"
Beth went on. "I happened to look up once, and such an expression as was on her face, girls! It was pathetic and sad and envious all at once. It really made me feel bad--for five minutes," she concluded honestly.

"Hasn't Miss Allen any friends at all?" asked Beth.

"No, I don't think she has," answered Jean. "She has lived here for fourteen years, so Mrs. Pickrell says. Think of that, girls! Fourteen years at Chestnut Terrace! Is it any wonder that she is thin and dried-up and snappy?"

"Nobody ever comes to see her and she never goes anywhere," said Beth.
"Dear me! She must feel lonely now when everybody else is being remembered by their friends. I can't forget her face tonight; it actually haunts me. Girls, how would you feel if you hadn't anyone belonging to you, and if nobody thought about you at Christmas?"

"Ow!" said Olive, as if the mere idea made her shiver.

A little silence followed. To tell the truth, none of them liked Miss Allen. They knew that she did not like them either, but considered them frivolous and pert, and complained when they made a racket.

"The skeleton at the feast," Jean called her, and certainly the presence of the pale, silent, discontented-looking woman at the No. 16 table did not tend to heighten its festivity.

Presently Jean said with a dramatic flourish, "Girls, I have an inspiration--a Christmas inspiration!"

"What is it?" cried four voices.

"Just this. Let us give Miss Allen a Christmas surprise. She has not received a single present and I'm sure she feels lonely. Just think how we would feel if we were in her place."

"That is true," said Olive thoughtfully. "Do you know, girls, this evening I went to her room with a message from Mrs. Pickrell, and I do believe she had been crying. Her room looked dreadfully bare and cheerless, too. I think she is very poor. What are we to do, Jean?"

"Let us each give her something nice. We can put the things just outside of her door so that she will see them whenever she opens it. I'll give her some of Fred's roses too, and I'll write a Christmassy letter in my very best style to go with them," said Jean, warming up to her ideas as she talked.

The other girls caught her spirit and entered into the plan with enthusiasm.
"Splendid!" cried Beth. "Jean, it is an inspiration, sure enough. Haven't we been horribly selfish--thinking of nothing but our own gifts and fun and pleasure? I really feel ashamed."
"Let us do the thing up the very best way we can," said Nellie, forgetting even her beloved chocolates in her eagerness. "The shops are open yet. Let us go up town and invest."

Five minutes later five capped and jacketed figures were scurrying up the street in the frosty, starlit December dusk. Miss Allen in her cold little room heard their gay voices and sighed. She was crying by herself in the dark. It was Christmas for everybody but her, she thought drearily.

In an hour the girls came back with their purchases.

"Now, let's hold a council of war," said Jean jubilantly. "I hadn't the faintest idea what Miss Allen would like so I just guessed wildly. I got her a lace handkerchief and a big bottle of perfume and a painted photograph frame--and I'll stick my own photo in it for fun. That was really all I could afford. Christmas purchases have left my purse dreadfully lean."

"I got her a glove-box and a pin tray," said Belle, "and Olive got her a calendar and Whittier's poems. And besides we are going to give her half of that big plummy fruit cake Mother sent us from home. I'm sure she hasn't tasted anything so delicious for years, for fruit cakes don't grow on Chestnut Terrace and she never goes anywhere else for a meal."

Beth had bought a pretty cup and saucer and said she meant to give one of her pretty water-colours too. Nellie, true to her reputation, had invested in a big box of chocolate creams, a gorgeously striped candy cane, a bag of oranges, and a brilliant lampshade of rose-coloured crepe paper to top off with.

"It makes such a lot of show for the money," she explained. "I am bankrupt, like Jean."

"Well, we've got a lot of pretty things," said Jean in a tone of satisfaction. "Now we must do them up nicely. Will you wrap them in tissue paper, girls, and tie them with baby ribbon-- here's a box of it--while I write that letter?" While the others chatted over their parcels Jean wrote her letter, and Jean could write delightful letters. She had a decided talent in that respect, and her correspondents all declared her letters to be things of beauty and joy forever. She put her best into Miss Allen's Christmas letter. Since then she has written many bright and clever things, but I do not believe she ever in her life wrote anything more genuinely original and delightful than that letter. Besides, it breathed the very spirit of Christmas, and all the girls declared that it was splendid.

"You must all sign it now," said Jean, "and I'll put it in one of those big envelopes; and, Nellie, won't you write her name on it in fancy letters?"

Which Nellie proceeded to do, and furthermore embellished the envelope by a border of chubby cherubs, dancing hand in hand around it and a sketch of No. 16 Chestnut Terrace in the corner in lieu of a stamp. Not content with this she hunted out a huge sheet of drawing paper and drew upon it an original pen-and-ink design after her own heart. A dudish cat--Miss Allen was fond of the No. 16 cat if she could be said to be fond of anything--was portrayed seated on a rocker arrayed in smoking jacket and cap with a cigar waved airily aloft in one paw while the other held out a placard bearing the legend "Merry Christmas." A second cat in full street costume bowed politely, hat in paw, and waved a banner inscribed with "Happy New Year," while faintly suggested kittens gambolled around the border. The girls laughed until they cried over it and voted it to be the best thing Nellie had yet done in original work.

All this had taken time and it was past eleven o'clock. Miss Allen had cried herself to sleep long ago and everybody else in Chestnut Terrace was abed when five figures cautiously crept down the hall, headed by Jean with a dim lamp. Outside of Miss Allen's door the procession halted and the girls silently arranged their gifts on the floor.

"That's done," whispered Jean in a tone of satisfaction as they tiptoed back. "And now let us go to bed or Mrs. Pickrell, bless her heart, will be down on us for burning so much midnight oil. Oil has gone up, you know, girls."

It was in the early morning that Miss Allen opened her door. But early as it was, another door down the hall was half open too and five rosy faces were peering cautiously out. The girls had been up for an hour for fear they would miss the sight and were all in Nellie's room, which commanded a view of Miss Allen's door.

That lady's face was a study. Amazement, incredulity, wonder, chased each other over it, succeeded by a glow of pleasure. On the floor before her was a snug little pyramid of parcels topped by Jean's letter. On a chair behind it was a bowl of delicious hot-house roses and Nellie's placard.

Miss Allen looked down the hall but saw nothing, for Jean had slammed the door just in time. Half an hour later when they were going down to breakfast Miss Allen came along the hall with outstretched hands to meet them. She had been crying again, but I think her tears were happy ones; and she was smiling now. A cluster of Jean's roses were pinned on her breast.

"Oh, girls, girls," she said, with a little tremble in her voice, "I can never thank you enough. It was so kind and sweet of you. You don't know how much good you have done me."

Breakfast was an unusually cheerful affair at No. 16 that morning. There was no skeleton at the feast and everybody was beaming. Miss Allen laughed and talked like a girl herself.

"Oh, how surprised I was!" she said. "The roses were like a bit of summer, and those cats of Nellie's were so funny and delightful. And your letter too, Jean! I cried and laughed over it. I shall read it every day for a year."

After breakfast everyone went to Christmas service. The girls went uptown to the church they attended. The city was very beautiful in the morning sunshine. There had been a white frost in the night and the tree-lined avenues and public squares seemed like glimpses of fairyland.

"How lovely the world is," said Jean.

"This is really the very happiest Christmas morning I have ever known," declared Nellie. "I never felt so really Christmassy in my inmost soul before."

"I suppose," said Beth thoughtfully, "that it is because we have discovered for ourselves the old truth that it is more blessed to give than to receive. I've always known it, in a way, but I never realized it before."

"Blessing on Jean's Christmas inspiration," said Nellie. "But, girls, let us try to make it an all-the-year-round inspiration, I say. We can bring a little of our own sunshine into Miss Allen's life as long as we live with her."

"Amen to that!" said Jean heartily. "Oh, listen, girls--the Christmas chimes!"

And over all the beautiful city was wafted the grand old message of peace on earth and good will to all the world.

A Christmas Mistake

"Tomorrow is Christmas," announced Teddy Grant exultantly, as he sat on the floor struggling manfully with a refractory bootlace that was knotted and tagless and stubbornly refused to go into the eyelets of Teddy's patched boots. "Ain't I glad, though. Hurrah!"

His mother was washing the breakfast dishes in a dreary, listless sort of way. She looked tired and broken-spirited. Ted's enthusiasm seemed to grate on her, for she answered sharply:

"Christmas, indeed. I can't see that it is anything for us to rejoice over. Other people may be glad enough, but what with winter coming on I'd sooner it was spring than Christmas. Mary Alice, do lift that child out of the ashes and put its shoes and stockings on. Everything seems to be at sixes and sevens here this morning."

Keith, the oldest boy, was coiled up on the sofa calmly working out some algebra problems, quite oblivious to the noise around him. But he looked up from his slate, with his pencil suspended above an obstinate equation, to declaim with a flourish:

"Christmas comes but once a year,
And then Mother wishes it wasn't here."

"I don't, then," said Gordon, son number two, who was preparing his own noon lunch of bread and molasses at the table, and making an atrocious mess of crumbs and sugary syrup over everything. "I know one thing to be thankful for, and that is that there'll be no school. We'll have a whole week of holidays."

Gordon was noted for his aversion to school and his affection for holidays.

"And we're going to have turkey for dinner," declared Teddy, getting up off the floor and rushing to secure his share of bread and molasses, "and cranb'ry sauce and--and--pound cake! Ain't we, Ma?"

"No, you are not," said Mrs. Grant desperately, dropping the dishcloth and snatching the baby on her knee to wipe the crust of cinders and molasses from the chubby pink-and-white face. "You may as well know it now, children, I've kept it from you so far in hopes that something would turn up, but nothing has. We can't have any Christmas dinner tomorrow--we can't afford it. I've pinched and saved every way I could for the last month, hoping that I'd be able to get a turkey for you anyhow, but you'll have to do without it. There's that doctor's bill to pay and a dozen other bills coming in--and people say they can't wait. I suppose they can't, but it's kind of hard, I must say."

The little Grants stood with open mouths and horrified eyes. No turkey for Christmas! Was the world coming to an end? Wouldn't the government interfere if anyone ventured to dispense with a Christmas celebration?

The gluttonous Teddy stuffed his fists into his eyes and lifted up his voice. Keith, who understood better than the others the look on his mother's face, took his blubbering young brother by the collar and marched him into the porch. The twins, seeing the summary proceeding, swallowed the outcries they had intended to make, although they couldn't keep a few big tears from running down their fat cheeks.

Mrs. Grant looked pityingly at the disappointed faces about her.
"Don't cry, children, you make me feel worse. We are not the only ones who will have to do without a Christmas turkey. We ought to be very thankful that we have anything to eat at all. I hate to disappoint you, but it can't be helped."

"Never mind, Mother," said Keith, comfortingly, relaxing his hold upon the porch door, whereupon it suddenly flew open and precipitated Teddy, who had been tugging at the handle, heels over head backwards. "We know you've done your best. It's been a hard year for you. Just wait, though. I'll soon be grown up, and then you and these greedy youngsters shall feast on turkey every day of the year. Hello, Teddy, have you got on your feet again? Mind, sir, no more blubbering!"

"When I'm a man," announced Teddy with dignity, "I'd just like to see you put me in the porch. And I mean to have turkey all the time and I won't give you any, either."

"All right, you greedy small boy. Only take yourself off to school now, and let us hear no more squeaks out of you. Tramp, all of you, and give Mother a chance to get her work done."

Mrs. Grant got up and fell to work at her dishes with a brighter face.

"Well, we mustn't give in; perhaps things will be better after a while. I'll make a famous bread pudding, and you can boil some molasses taffy and ask those little Smithsons next door to help you pull it. They won't whine for turkey, I'll be bound. I don't suppose they ever tasted such a thing in all their lives. If I could afford it, I'd have had them all in to dinner with us. That sermon Mr. Evans preached last Sunday kind of stirred me up. He said we ought always to try and share our Christmas joy with some poor souls who had never learned the meaning of the word. I can't do as much as I'd like to. It was different when your father was alive."

The noisy group grew silent as they always did when their father was spoken of. He had died the year before, and since his death the little family had had a hard time. Keith, to hide his feelings, began to hector the rest.

"Mary Alice, do hurry up. Here, you twin nuisances, get off to school. If you don't you'll be late and then the master will give you a whipping."

"He won't," answered the irrepressible Teddy. "He never whips us, he doesn't. He stands us on the floor sometimes, though," he added, remembering the many times his own chubby legs had been seen to better advantage on the school platform.

"That man," said Mrs. Grant, alluding to the teacher, "makes me nervous. He is the most abstracted creature I ever saw in my life. It is a wonder to me he doesn't walk straight into the river some day. You'll meet him meandering along the street, gazing into vacancy, and he'll never see you nor hear a word you say half the time."

"Yesterday," said Gordon, chuckling over the remembrance, "he came in with a big piece of paper he'd picked up on the entry floor in one hand and his hat in the other--and he stuffed his hat into the coal-scuttle and hung up the paper on a nail as grave as you please. Never knew the difference till Ned Slocum went and told him. He's always doing things like that."

Keith had collected his books and now marched his brothers and sisters off to school. Left alone with the baby, Mrs. Grant betook herself to her work with a heavy heart. But a second interruption broke the progress of her dish-washing.

"I declare," she said, with a surprised glance through the window, "if there isn't that absent-minded schoolteacher coming through the yard!
What can he want? Dear me, I do hope Teddy hasn't been cutting capers in school again."

For the teacher's last call had been in October and had been occasioned by the fact that the irrepressible Teddy would persist in going to school with his pockets filled with live crickets and in driving them harnessed to strings up and down the aisle when the teacher's back was turned. All mild methods of punishment having failed, the teacher had called to talk it over with Mrs. Grant, with the happy result that Teddy's behaviour had improved--in the matter of crickets at least.

But it was about time for another outbreak. Teddy had been unnaturally good for too long a time. Poor Mrs. Grant feared that it was the calm before a storm, and it was with nervous haste that she went to the door and greeted the young teacher.

He was a slight, pale, boyish-looking fellow, with an abstracted, musing look in his large dark eyes. Mrs. Grant noticed with amusement that he wore a white straw hat in spite of the season. His eyes were directed to her face with his usual unseeing gaze.

"Just as though he was looking through me at something a thousand miles away," said Mrs. Grant afterwards. "I believe he was, too. His body was right there on the step before me, but where his soul was is more than you or I or anybody can tell."

"Good morning," he said absently. "I have just called on my way to school with a message from Miss Millar. She wants you all to come up and have Christmas dinner with her tomorrow."

"For the land's sake!" said Mrs. Grant blankly. "I don't understand."
To herself she thought, "I wish I dared take him and shake him to find if he's walking in his sleep or not."

"You and all the children--every one," went on the teacher dreamily, as if he were reciting a lesson learned beforehand. "She told me to tell you to be sure and come. Shall I say that you will?"

"Oh, yes, that is--I suppose--I don't know," said Mrs. Grant incoherently. "I never expected--yes, you may tell her we'll come," she concluded abruptly.

"Thank you," said the abstracted messenger, gravely lifting his hat and looking squarely through Mrs. Grant into unknown regions. When he had gone Mrs. Grant went in and sat down, laughing in a sort of hysterical way.

"I wonder if it is all right. Could Cornelia really have told him? She must, I suppose, but it is enough to take one's breath."

Mrs. Grant and Cornelia Millar were cousins, and had once been the closest of friends, but that was years ago, before some spiteful reports and ill-natured gossip had come between them, making only a little rift at first that soon widened into a chasm of coldness and alienation. Therefore this invitation surprised Mrs. Grant greatly.

Miss Cornelia was a maiden lady of certain years, with a comfortable bank account and a handsome, old-fashioned house on the hill behind the village. She always boarded the schoolteachers and looked after them maternally; she was an active church worker and a tower of strength to struggling ministers and their families.

"If Cornelia has seen fit at last to hold out the hand of reconciliation I'm glad enough to take it. Dear knows, I've wanted to make up often enough, but I didn't think she ever would. We've both of us got too much pride and stubbornness. It's the Turner blood in us that does it. The Turners were all so set. But I mean to do my part now she has done hers."

And Mrs. Grant made a final attack on the dishes with a beaming face.

When the little Grants came home and heard the news, Teddy stood on his head to express his delight, the twins kissed each other, and Mary Alice and Gordon danced around the kitchen.

Keith thought himself too big to betray any joy over a Christmas dinner, but he whistled while doing the chores until the bare welkin in the yard rang, and Teddy, in spite of unheard of misdemeanours, was not collared off into the porch once.

When the young teacher got home from school that evening he found the yellow house full of all sorts of delectable odours. Miss Cornelia herself was concocting mince pies after the famous family recipe, while her ancient and faithful handmaiden, Hannah, was straining into moulds the cranberry jelly. The open pantry door revealed a tempting array of Christmas delicacies.

"Did you call and invite the Smithsons up to dinner as I told you?" asked Miss Cornelia anxiously.

"Yes," was the dreamy response as he glided through the kitchen and vanished into the hall.

Miss Cornelia crimped the edges of her pies delicately with a relieved air. "I made certain he'd forget it," she said. "You just have to watch him as if he were a mere child. Didn't I catch him yesterday starting off to school in his carpet slippers? And in spite of me he got away today in that ridiculous summer hat. You'd better set that jelly in the out-pantry to cool, Hannah; it looks good. We'll give those poor little Smithsons a feast for once in their lives if they never get another."

At this juncture the hall door flew open and Mr. Palmer appeared on the threshold. He seemed considerably agitated and for once his eyes had lost their look of space-searching.

"Miss Millar, I am afraid I did make a mistake this morning--it has just dawned on me. I am almost sure that I called at Mrs. Grant's and invited her and her family instead of the Smithsons. And she said they would come."

Miss Cornelia's face was a study.

"Mr. Palmer," she said, flourishing her crimping fork tragically, "do you mean to say you went and invited Linda Grant here tomorrow? Linda Grant, of all women in this world!"

"I did," said the teacher with penitent wretchedness. "It was very careless of me--I am very sorry. What can I do? I'll go down and tell them I made a mistake if you like."

"You can't do that," groaned Miss Cornelia, sitting down and wrinkling up her forehead in dire perplexity. "It would never do in the world. For pity's sake, let me think for a minute."

Miss Cornelia did think--to good purpose evidently, for her forehead smoothed out as her meditations proceeded and her face brightened. Then she got up briskly. "Well, you've done it and no mistake. I don't know that I'm sorry, either. Anyhow, we'll leave it as it is. But you must go straight down now and invite the Smithsons too. And for pity's sake, don't make any more mistakes."

When he had gone Miss Cornelia opened her heart to Hannah. "I never could have done it myself--never; the Turner is too strong in me. But I'm glad it is done. I've been wanting for years to make up with Linda. And now the chance has come, thanks to that blessed blundering boy, I mean to make the most of it. Mind, Hannah, you never whisper a word about its being a mistake. Linda must never know. Poor Linda!

She's had a hard time. Hannah, we must make some more pies, and I must go straight down to the store and get some more Santa Claus stuff;

I've only got enough to go around the Smithsons."

When Mrs. Grant and her family arrived at the yellow house next morning Miss Cornelia herself ran out bareheaded to meet them. The two women shook hands a little stiffly and then a rill of long-repressed affection trickled out from some secret spring in Miss Cornelia's heart and she kissed her new-found old friend tenderly. Linda returned the kiss warmly, and both felt that the old-time friendship was theirs again.

The little Smithsons all came and they and the little Grants sat down on the long bright dining room to a dinner that made history in their small lives, and was eaten over again in happy dreams for months.

How those children did eat! And how beaming Miss Cornelia and grim-faced, soft-hearted Hannah and even the absent-minded teacher himself enjoyed watching them!

After dinner Miss Cornelia distributed among the delighted little souls the presents she had bought for them, and then turned them loose in the big shining kitchen to have a taffy pull--and they had it to their hearts' content! And as for the shocking, taffyfied state into which they got their own rosy faces and that once immaculate domain--well, as Miss Cornelia and Hannah never said one word about it, neither will I.

The four women enjoyed the afternoon in their own way, and the schoolteacher buried himself in algebra to his own great satisfaction.

When her guests went home in the starlit December dusk, Miss Cornelia walked part of the way with them and had a long confidential talk with Mrs. Grant. When she returned it was to find Hannah groaning in and over the kitchen and the schoolteacher dreamily trying to clean some molasses off his boots with the kitchen hairbrush. Long-suffering Miss Cornelia rescued her property and despatched Mr. Palmer into the woodshed to find the shoe-brush. Then she sat down and laughed.

"Hannah, what will become of that boy yet? There's no counting on what he'll do next. I don't know how he'll ever get through the world, I'm sure, but I'll look after him while he's here at least. I owe him a huge debt of gratitude for this Christmas blunder. What an awful mess this place is in! But, Hannah, did you ever in the world see anything so delightful as that little Tommy Smithson stuffing himself with plum cake, not to mention Teddy Grant? It did me good just to see them."

Aunt Cyrilla's Christmas Basket

When Lucy Rose met Aunt Cyrilla coming downstairs, somewhat flushed and breathless from her ascent to the garret, with a big, flat-covered basket hanging over her plump arm, she gave a little sigh of despair. Lucy Rose had done her brave best for some years--in fact, ever since she had put up her hair and lengthened her skirts--to break Aunt Cyrilla of the habit of carrying that basket with her every time she went to Pembroke; but Aunt Cyrilla still insisted on taking it, and only laughed at what she called Lucy Rose's "finicky notions." Lucy Rose had a horrible, haunting idea that it was extremely provincial for her aunt always to take the big basket, packed full of country good things, whenever she went to visit Edward and Geraldine. Geraldine was so stylish, and might think it queer; and then Aunt Cyrilla always would carry it on her arm and give cookies and apples and molasses taffy out of it to every child she encountered and, just as often as not, to older folks too. Lucy Rose, when she went to town with Aunt Cyrilla, felt chagrined over this--all of which goes to prove that Lucy was as yet very young and had a great deal to learn in this world.

That troublesome worry over what Geraldine would think nerved her to make a protest in this instance.

"Now, Aunt C'rilla," she pleaded, "you're surely not going to take that funny old basket to Pembroke this time--Christmas Day and all."

"'Deed and 'deed I am," returned Aunt Cyrilla briskly, as she put it on the table and proceeded to dust it out. "I never went to see Edward and Geraldine since they were married that I didn't take a basket of good things along with me for them, and I'm not going to stop now. As for it's being Christmas, all the more reason. Edward is always real glad to get some of the old farmhouse goodies. He says they beat city cooking all hollow, and so they do."

"But it's so countrified," moaned Lucy Rose.

"Well, I am countrified," said Aunt Cyrilla firmly, "and so are you. And what's more, I don't see that it's anything to be ashamed of. You've got some real silly pride about you, Lucy Rose. You'll grow out of it in time, but just now it is giving you a lot of trouble."

"The basket is a lot of trouble," said Lucy Rose crossly. "You're always mislaying it or afraid you will. And it does look so funny to be walking through the streets with that big, bulgy basket hanging on your arm."

"I'm not a mite worried about its looks," returned Aunt Cyrilla calmly. "As for its being a trouble, why, maybe it is, but I have that, and other people have the pleasure of it. Edward and Geraldine don't need it--I know that--but there may be those that will. And if it hurts your feelings to walk 'longside of a countrified old lady with a countrified basket, why, you can just fall behind, as it were."

Aunt Cyrilla nodded and smiled good-humouredly, and Lucy Rose, though she privately held to her own opinion, had to smile too.

"Now, let me see," said Aunt Cyrilla reflectively, tapping the snowy kitchen table with the point of her plump, dimpled forefinger, "what shall I take? That big fruit cake for one thing--Edward does like my fruit cake; and that cold boiled tongue for another. Those three mince pies too, they'd spoil before we got back or your uncle'd make himself sick eating them--mince pie is his besetting sin. And that little stone bottle full of cream--Geraldine may carry any amount of style, but I've yet to see her look down on real good country cream, Lucy Rose; and another bottle of my raspberry vinegar. That plate of jelly cookies and doughnuts will please the children and fill up the chinks, and you can bring me that box of ice-cream candy out of the pantry, and that bag of striped candy sticks your uncle brought home from the corner last night. And apples, of course--three or four dozen of those good eaters--and a little pot of my greengage preserves--Edward'll like that. And some sandwiches and pound cake for a snack for ourselves. Now, I guess that will do for eatables. The presents for the children can go in on top. There's a doll for Daisy and the little boat your uncle made for Ray and a tatted lace handkerchief apiece for the twins, and the crochet hood for the baby. Now, is that all?"

"There's a cold roast chicken in the pantry," said Lucy Rose wickedly, "and the pig Uncle Leo killed is hanging up in the porch. Couldn't you put them in too?"

Aunt Cyrilla smiled broadly. "Well, I guess we'll leave the pig alone; but since you have reminded me of it, the chicken may as well go in. I can make room."

Lucy Rose, in spite of her prejudices, helped with the packing and, not having been trained under Aunt Cyrilla's eye for nothing, did it very well too, with much clever economy of space. But when Aunt Cyrilla had put in as a finishing touch a big bouquet of pink and white everlastings, and tied the bulging covers down with a firm hand, Lucy Rose stood over the basket and whispered vindictively:

"Some day I'm going to burn this basket--when I get courage enough. Then there'll be an end of lugging it everywhere we go like a--like an old market-woman."

Uncle Leopold came in just then, shaking his head dubiously. He was not going to spend Christmas with Edward and Geraldine, and perhaps the prospect of having to cook and eat his Christmas dinner all alone made him pessimistic.

"I mistrust you folks won't get to Pembroke tomorrow," he said sagely.
"It's going to storm."

Aunt Cyrilla did not worry over this. She believed matters of this kind were fore-ordained, and she slept calmly. But Lucy Rose got up three times in the night to see if it were storming, and when she did sleep had horrible nightmares of struggling through blinding snowstorms dragging Aunt Cyrilla's Christmas basket along with her.

It was not snowing in the early morning, and Uncle Leopold drove Aunt Cyrilla and Lucy Rose and the basket to the station, four miles off. When they reached there the air was thick with flying flakes. The stationmaster sold them their tickets with a grim face.

"If there's any more snow comes, the trains might as well keep

Christmas too," he said. "There's been so much snow already that traffic is blocked half the time, and now there ain't no place to shovel the snow off onto."

Aunt Cyrilla said that if the train were to get to Pembroke in time for Christmas, it would get there; and she opened her basket and gave the stationmaster and three small boys an apple apiece.

"That's the beginning," groaned Lucy Rose to herself.

When their train came along Aunt Cyrilla established herself in one seat and her basket in another, and looked beamingly around her at her fellow travellers.

These were few in number--a delicate little woman at the end of the car, with a baby and four other children, a young girl across the aisle with a pale, pretty face, a sunburned lad three seats ahead in a khaki uniform, a very handsome, imposing old lady in a sealskin coat ahead of him, and a thin young man with spectacles opposite.

"A minister," reflected Aunt Cyrilla, beginning to classify, "who takes better care of other folks' souls than of his own body; and that woman in the sealskin is discontented and cross at something — got up too early to catch the train, maybe; and that young chap must be one of the boys not long out of the hospital. That woman's children look as if they hadn't enjoyed a square meal since they were born; and if that girl across from me has a mother, I'd like to know what the woman means, letting her daughter go from home in this weather in clothes like that."

Lucy Rose merely wondered uncomfortably what the others thought of Aunt Cyrilla's basket.

They expected to reach Pembroke that night, but as the day wore on the storm grew worse. Twice the train had to stop while the train hands dug it out. The third time it could not go on. It was dusk when the conductor came through the train, replying brusquely to the questions of the anxious passengers.

"A nice lookout for Christmas--no, impossible to go on or back — track blocked for miles--what's that, madam?--no, no station near--woods for miles. We're here for the night. These storms of late have played the mischief with everything."

"Oh, dear," groaned Lucy Rose.

Aunt Cyrilla looked at her basket complacently. "At any rate, we won't starve," she said.

The pale, pretty girl seemed indifferent. The sealskin lady looked crosser than ever. The khaki boy said, "Just my luck," and two of the children began to cry. Aunt Cyrilla took some apples and striped candy sticks from her basket and carried them to them. She lifted the oldest into her ample lap and soon had them all around her, laughing and contented.

The rest of the travellers straggled over to the corner and drifted into conversation. The khaki boy said it was hard lines not to get home for Christmas, after all.

"I was invalided from South Africa three months ago, and I've been in the hospital at Netley ever since. Reached Halifax three days ago and telegraphed the old folks I'd eat my Christmas dinner with them, and to have an extra-big turkey because I didn't have any last year. They'll be badly disappointed."

He looked disappointed too. One khaki sleeve hung empty by his side. Aunt Cyrilla passed him an apple.

"We were all going down to Grandpa's for Christmas," said the little mother's oldest boy dolefully. "We've never been there before, and it's just too bad."

He looked as if he wanted to cry but thought better of it and bit off a mouthful of candy.

"Will there be any Santa Claus on the train?" demanded his small sister tearfully. "Jack says there won't."

"I guess he'll find you out," said Aunt Cyrilla reassuringly.

The pale, pretty girl came up and took the baby from the tired mother.
"What a dear little fellow," she said softly.

"Are you going home for Christmas too?" asked Aunt Cyrilla.

The girl shook her head. "I haven't any home. I'm just a shop girl out of work at present, and I'm going to Pembroke to look for some."

Aunt Cyrilla went to her basket and took out her box of cream candy.
"I guess we might as well enjoy ourselves. Let's eat it all up and have a good time. Maybe we'll get down to Pembroke in the morning."

The little group grew cheerful as they nibbled, and even the pale girl brightened up. The little mother told Aunt Cyrilla her story aside.

She had been long estranged from her family, who had disapproved of her marriage. Her husband had died the previous summer, leaving her in poor circumstances.

"Father wrote to me last week and asked me to let bygones be bygones and come home for Christmas. I was so glad. And the children's hearts were set on it. It seems too bad that we are not to get there. I have to be back at work the morning after Christmas."

The khaki boy came up again and shared the candy. He told amusing stories of campaigning in South Africa. The minister came too, and listened, and even the sealskin lady turned her head over her shoulder.

By and by the children fell asleep, one on Aunt Cyrilla's lap and one on Lucy Rose's, and two on the seat. Aunt Cyrilla and the pale girl helped the mother make up beds for them. The minister gave his overcoat and the sealskin lady came forward with a shawl.

"This will do for the baby," she said.

"We must get up some Santa Claus for these youngsters," said the khaki boy. "Let's hang their stockings on the wall and fill 'em up as best we can. I've nothing about me but some hard cash and a jack-knife. I'll give each of 'em a quarter and the boy can have the knife."

"I've nothing but money either," said the sealskin lady regretfully.

Aunt Cyrilla glanced at the little mother. She had fallen asleep with her head against the seat-back.

"I've got a basket over there," said Aunt Cyrilla firmly, "and I've some presents in it that I was taking to my nephew's children. I'm going to give 'em to these. As for the money, I think the mother is the one for it to go to. She's been telling me her story, and a pitiful one it is. Let's make up a little purse among us for a Christmas present."

The idea met with favour. The khaki boy passed his cap and everybody contributed. The sealskin lady put in a crumpled note. When Aunt Cyrilla straightened it out she saw that it was for twenty dollars.

Meanwhile, Lucy Rose had brought the basket. She smiled at Aunt Cyrilla as she lugged it down the aisle and Aunt Cyrilla smiled back. Lucy Rose had never touched that basket of her own accord before.

Ray's boat went to Jacky, and Daisy's doll to his oldest sister, the twins' lace handkerchiefs to the two smaller girls and the hood to the baby. Then the stockings were filled up with doughnuts and jelly cookies and the money was put in an envelope and pinned to the little mother's jacket.

"That baby is such a dear little fellow," said the sealskin lady gently. "He looks something like my little son. He died eighteen Christmases ago."

Aunt Cyrilla put her hand over the lady's kid glove. "So did mine," she said. Then the two women smiled tenderly at each other. Afterwards they rested from their labours and all had what Aunt Cyrilla called a "snack" of sandwiches and pound cake. The khaki boy said he hadn't tasted anything half so good since he left home.

"They didn't give us pound cake in South Africa," he said.

When morning came the storm was still raging. The children wakened and went wild with delight over their stockings. The little mother found her envelope and tried to utter thanks and broke down; and nobody knew what to say or do, when the conductor fortunately came in and made a diversion by telling them they might as well resign themselves to spending Christmas on the train.

"This is serious," said the khaki boy, "when you consider that we've no provisions. Don't mind for myself, used to half rations or no rations at all. But these kiddies will have tremendous appetites."

Then Aunt Cyrilla rose to the occasion.

"I've got some emergency rations here," she announced. "There's plenty for all and we'll have our Christmas dinner, although a cold one.
Breakfast first thing. There's a sandwich apiece left and we must fill up on what is left of the cookies and doughnuts and save the rest for a real good spread at dinner time. The only thing is, I haven't any bread."

"I've a box of soda crackers," said the little mother eagerly.

Nobody in that car will ever forget that Christmas. To begin with, after breakfast they had a concert. The khaki boy gave two recitations, sang three songs, and gave a whistling solo. Lucy Rose gave three recitations and the minister a comic reading. The pale shop girl sang two songs. It was agreed that the khaki boy's whistling solo was the best number, and Aunt Cyrilla gave him the bouquet of everlastings as a reward of merit.

Then the conductor came in with the cheerful news that the storm was almost over and he thought the track would be cleared in a few hours.

"If we can get to the next station we'll be all right," he said. "The branch joins the main line there and the tracks will be clear."

At noon they had dinner. The train hands were invited in to share it. The minister carved the chicken with the brakeman's jack-knife and the khaki boy cut up the tongue and the mince pies, while the sealskin lady mixed the raspberry vinegar with its due proportion of water. Bits of paper served as plates. The train furnished a couple of glasses, a tin pint cup was discovered and given to the children, Aunt Cyrilla and Lucy Rose and the sealskin lady drank, turn about, from the latter's graduated medicine glass, the shop girl and the little mother shared one of the empty bottles, and the khaki boy, the minister, and the train men drank out of the other bottle.

Everybody declared they had never enjoyed a meal more in their lives. Certainly it was a merry one, and Aunt Cyrilla's cooking was never more appreciated; indeed, the bones of the chicken and the pot of preserves were all that was left. They could not eat the preserves because they had no spoons, so Aunt Cyrilla gave them to the little mother.

When all was over, a hearty vote of thanks was passed to Aunt Cyrilla and her basket. The sealskin lady wanted to know how she made her pound cake, and the khaki boy asked for her receipt for jelly cookies. And when two hours later the conductor came in and said the snowploughs had got along and they'd soon be starting, they all wondered if it could really be less than twenty-four hours since they met.

"I feel as if I'd been campaigning with you all my life," said the khaki boy.

At the next station they all parted. The little mother and the children had to take the next train back home. The minister stayed there, and the khaki boy and the sealskin lady changed trains. The sealskin lady shook Aunt Cyrilla's hand. She no longer looked discontented or cross.

"This has been the pleasantest Christmas I have ever spent," she said heartily. "I shall never forget that wonderful basket of yours. The little shop girl is going home with me. I've promised her a place in my husband's store."

When Aunt Cyrilla and Lucy Rose reached Pembroke there was nobody to meet them because everyone had given up expecting them. It was not far from the station to Edward's house and Aunt Cyrilla elected to walk.

"I'll carry the basket," said Lucy Rose.

Aunt Cyrilla relinquished it with a smile. Lucy Rose smiled too.

"It's a blessed old basket," said the latter, "and I love it. Please forget all the silly things I ever said about it, Aunt C'rilla."

The Josephs' Christmas

The month before Christmas was always the most exciting and mysterious time in the Joseph household. Such scheming and planning, such putting of curly heads together in corners, such counting of small hoards, such hiding and smuggling of things out of sight, as went on among the little Josephs!

There were a good many of them, and very few of the pennies; hence the reason for so much contriving and consulting. From fourteen-year-old Mollie down to four-year-old Lennie there were eight small Josephs in all in the little log house on the prairie; so that when each little Joseph wanted to give a Christmas box to each of the other little Josephs, and something to Father and Mother Joseph besides, it is no wonder that they had to cudgel their small brains for ways and means thereof.

Father and Mother were always discreetly blind and silent through December. No questions were asked no matter what queer things were done. Many secret trips to the little store at the railway station two miles away were ignored, and no little Joseph was called to account because he or she looked terribly guilty when somebody suddenly came into the room. The air was simply charged with secrets.

Sister Mollie was the grand repository of these; all the little Josephs came to her for advice and assistance. It was Mollie who for troubled small brothers and sisters did such sums in division as this:

How can I get a ten-cent present for Emmy and a fifteen-cent one for Jimmy out of eighteen cents? Or, how can seven sticks of candy be divided among eight people so that each shall have one? It was Mollie who advised regarding the purchase of ribbon and crepe paper. It was Mollie who put the finishing touches to most of the little gifts. In short, all through December Mollie was weighed down under an avalanche of responsibility. It speaks volumes for her sagacity and skill that she never got things mixed up or made any such terrible mistake as letting one little Joseph find out what another was going to give him. "Dead" secrecy was the keystone of all plans and confidences.

During this particular December the planning and contriving had been more difficult and the results less satisfactory than usual. The Josephs were poor at any time, but this winter they were poorer than ever. The crops had failed in the summer, and as a consequence the family were, as Jimmy said, "on short commons." But they made the brave best of their small resources, and on Christmas Eve every little Joseph went to bed with a clear conscience, for was there not on the corner table in the kitchen a small mountain of tiny--sometimes very tiny--gifts labelled with the names of recipients and givers, and worth their weight in gold if love and good wishes count for anything?

It was beginning to snow when the small small Josephs went to bed, and when the big small Josephs climbed the stairs it was snowing thickly. Mr. and Mrs. Joseph sat before the fire and listened to the wind howling about the house.

"I'm glad I'm not driving over the prairie tonight," said Mr. Joseph.

"It's quite a storm. I hope it will be fine tomorrow, for the children's sake. They've set their hearts on having a sleigh ride, and it will be too bad if they can't have it when it's about all the Christmas they'll have this year. Mary, this is the first Christmas since we came west that we couldn't afford some little extras for them, even if 'twas only a box of nuts and candy."

Mrs. Joseph sighed over Jimmy's worn jacket which she was mending. Then she smiled.

"Never mind, John. Things will be better next Christmas, we'll hope. The children will not mind, bless their hearts. Look at all the little knick-knacks they've made for each other. Last week when I was over at Taunton, Mr. Fisher had his store all gayified up,' as Jim says, with Christmas presents. I did feel that I'd ask nothing better than to go in and buy all the lovely things I wanted, just for once, and give them to the children tomorrow morning. They've never had anything really nice for Christmas. But there! We've all got each other and good health and spirits, and a Christmas wouldn't be much without those if we had all the presents in the world."

Mr. Joseph nodded.

"That's so. I don't want to grumble; but I tell you I did want to get Maggie a 'real live doll,' as she calls it. She never has had anything but homemade dolls, and that small heart of hers is set on a real one. There was one at Fisher's store today--a big beauty with real hair, and eyes that opened and shut. Just fancy Maggie's face if she saw such a Christmas box as that tomorrow morning."

"Don't let's fancy it," laughed Mrs. Joseph, "it is only aggravating.

Talking of candy reminds me that I made a big plateful of taffy for the children today. It's all the 'Christmassy' I could give them. I'll get it out and put it on the table along with the children's presents. That can't be someone at the door!"

"It is, though," said Mr. Joseph as he strode to the door and flung it open.

Two snowed-up figures were standing on the porch. As they stepped in, the Josephs recognized one of them as Mr. Ralston, a wealthy merchant in a small town fifteen miles away.

"Late hour for callers, isn't it?" said Mr. Ralston. "The fact is, our horse has about given out, and the storm is so bad that we can't proceed. This is my wife, and we are on our way to spend Christmas with my brother's family at Lindsay. Can you take us in for the night, Mr. Joseph?"

"Certainly, and welcome!" exclaimed Mr. Joseph heartily, "if you don't mind a shakedown by the kitchen fire for the night. My, Mrs. Ralston," as his wife helped her off with her things, "but you are snowed up! I'll see to putting your horse away, Mr. Ralston. This way, if you please."

When the two men came stamping into the house again Mrs. Ralston and Mrs. Joseph were sitting at the fire, the former with a steaming hot cup of tea in her hand. Mr. Ralston put the big basket he was carrying down on a bench in the corner.

"Thought I'd better bring our Christmas flummery in," he said. "You see, Mrs. Joseph, my brother has a big family, so we are taking them a lot of Santa Claus stuff. Mrs. Ralston packed this basket, and goodness knows what she put in it, but she half cleaned out my store.

The eyes of the Lindsay youngsters will dance tomorrow--that is, if we ever get there."

Mrs. Joseph gave a little sigh in spite of herself, and looked wistfully at the heap of gifts on the corner table. How meagre and small they did look, to be sure, beside that bulgy basket with its cover suggestively tied down.

Mrs. Ralston looked too.

"Santa Claus seems to have visited you already," she said with a smile.

The Josephs laughed.

"Our Santa Claus is somewhat out of pocket this year," said Mr. Joseph frankly. "Those are the little things the small folks here have made for each other. They've been a month at it, and I'm always kind of relieved when Christmas is over and there are no more mysterious doings. We're in such cramped quarters here that you can't move without stepping on somebody's secret."

A shakedown was spread in the kitchen for the unexpected guests, and presently the Ralstons found themselves alone. Mrs. Ralston went over to the Christmas table and looked at the little gifts half tenderly and half pityingly.

"They're not much like the contents of our basket, are they?" she said, as she touched the calendar Jimmie had made for Mollie out of cardboard and autumn leaves and grasses.

"Just what I was thinking," returned her husband, "and I was thinking of something else, too. I've a notion that I'd like to see some of the things in our basket right here on this table."

"I'd like to see them all," said Mrs. Ralston promptly. "Let's just leave them here, Edward. Roger's family will have plenty of presents without them, and for that matter we can send them ours when we go back home."

"Just as you say," agreed Mr. Ralston. "I like the idea of giving the small folk of this household a rousing good Christmas for once. They're poor I know, and I dare say pretty well pinched this year like most of the farmers hereabout after the crop failure."

Mrs. Ralston untied the cover of the big basket. Then the two of them, moving as stealthily as if engaged in a burglary, transferred the contents to the table. Mr. Ralston got out a small pencil and a note book, and by dint of comparing the names attached to the gifts on the table they managed to divide theirs up pretty evenly among the little Josephs.

When all was done Mrs. Ralston said, "Now, I'm going to spread that tablecloth carelessly over the table. We will be going before daylight, probably, and in the hurry of getting off I hope that Mr. and Mrs. Joseph will not notice the difference till we're gone."

It fell out as Mrs. Ralston had planned. The dawn broke fine and clear over a vast white world. Mr. and Mrs. Joseph were early astir; breakfast for the storm-stayed travellers was cooked and eaten by lamplight; then the horse and sleigh were brought to the door and Mr. Ralston carried out his empty basket.

"I expect the trail will be heavy," he said, "but I guess we'd get to Lindsay in time for dinner, anyway. Much obliged for your kindness, Mr. Joseph. When you and Mrs. Joseph come to town we shall hope to have a chance to return it. Good-bye and a merry Christmas to you all."

When Mrs. Joseph went back to the kitchen her eyes fell on the heaped-up table in the corner.

"Why-y!" she said, and snatched off the cover.

One look she gave, and then this funny little mother began to cry; but they were happy tears. Mr. Joseph came too, and looked and whistled.

There really seemed to be everything on that table that the hearts of children could desire--three pairs of skates, a fur cap and collar, a dainty workbasket, half a dozen gleaming new books, a writing desk, a roll of stuff that looked like a new dress, a pair of fur-topped kid gloves just Mollie's size, and a china cup and saucer. All these were to be seen at the first glance; and in one corner of the table was a big box filled with candies and nuts and raisins, and in the other a doll with curling golden hair and brown eyes, dressed in "real" clothes and with all her wardrobe in a trunk beside her. Pinned to her dress was a leaf from Mr. Ralston's notebook with Maggie's name written on it.

"Well, this is Christmas with a vengeance," said Mr. Joseph.

"The children will go wild with delight," said his wife happily.

They pretty nearly did when they all came scrambling down the stairs a little later. Such a Christmas had never been known in the Joseph household before. Maggie clasped her doll with shining eyes, Mollie looked at the workbasket that her housewifely little heart had always longed for, studious Jimmy beamed over the books, and Ted and Hal whooped with delight over the skates. And as for the big box of good things, why, everybody appreciated that. That Christmas was one to date from in that family.

I'm glad to be able to say, too, that even in the heyday of their delight and surprise over their wonderful presents, the little Josephs did not forget to appreciate the gifts they had prepared for each other. Mollie thought her calendar just too pretty for anything, and Jimmy was sure the new red mittens which Maggie had knitted for him with her own chubby wee fingers, were the very nicest, gayest mittens a boy had ever worn.

Mrs. Joseph's taffy was eaten too. Not a scrap of it was left. As Ted said loyally, "It was just as good as the candy in the box and had more 'chew' to it besides."

The Osbornes' Christmas

Cousin Myra had come to spend Christmas at "The Firs," and all the junior Osbornes were ready to stand on their heads with delight.
Darby--whose real name was Charles--did it, because he was only eight, and at eight you have no dignity to keep up. The others, being older, couldn't.

But the fact of Christmas itself awoke no great enthusiasm in the hearts of the junior Osbornes. Frank voiced their opinion of it the day after Cousin Myra had arrived. He was sitting on the table with his hands in his pockets and a cynical sneer on his face. At least, Frank flattered himself that it was cynical. He knew that Uncle Edgar was said to wear a cynical sneer, and Frank admired Uncle Edgar very much and imitated him in every possible way. But to you and me it would have looked just as it did to Cousin Myra--a very discontented and unbecoming scowl.

"I'm awfully glad to see you, Cousin Myra," explained Frank carefully, "and your being here may make some things worth while. But Christmas is just a bore--a regular bore."

That was what Uncle Edgar called things that didn't interest him, so that Frank felt pretty sure of his word. Nevertheless, he wondered uncomfortably what made Cousin Myra smile so queerly.

"Why, how dreadful!" she said brightly. "I thought all boys and girls looked upon Christmas as the very best time in the year."

"We don't," said Frank gloomily. "It's just the same old thing year in and year out. We know just exactly what is going to happen. We even know pretty well what presents we are going to get. And Christmas Day itself is always the same. We'll get up in the morning, and our stockings will be full of things, and half of them we don't want. Then there's dinner. It's always so poky. And all the uncles and aunts come to dinner--just the same old crowd, every year, and they say just the same things. Aunt Desda always says, 'Why, Frankie, how you have grown!' She knows I hate to be called Frankie. And after dinner they'll sit round and talk the rest of the day, and that's all. Yes, I call Christmas a nuisance."

"There isn't a single bit of fun in it," said Ida discontentedly.

"Not a bit!" said the twins, both together, as they always said things.
"There's lots of candy," said Darby stoutly. He rather liked Christmas, although he was ashamed to say so before Frank.

Cousin Myra smothered another of those queer smiles.

"You've had too much Christmas, you Osbornes," she said seriously. "It has palled on your taste, as all good things will if you overdo them. Did you ever try giving Christmas to somebody else?"

The Osbornes looked at Cousin Myra doubtfully. They didn't understand.

"We always send presents to all our cousins," said Frank hesitatingly.

"That's a bore, too. They've all got so many things already it's no end of bother to think of something new."

"That isn't what I mean," said Cousin Myra. "How much Christmas do you suppose those little Rolands down there in the hollow have? Or Sammy Abbott with his lame back? Or French Joe's family over the hill? If you have too much Christmas, why don't you give some to them?"

The Osbornes looked at each other. This was a new idea.

"How could we do it?" asked Ida.

Whereupon they had a consultation. Cousin Myra explained her plan, and the Osbornes grew enthusiastic over it. Even Frank forgot that he was supposed to be wearing a cynical sneer.

"I move we do it, Osbornes," said he.

"If Father and Mother are willing," said Ida.

"Won't it be jolly!" exclaimed the twins.

"Well, rather," said Darby scornfully. He did not mean to be scornful. He had heard Frank saying the same words in the same tone, and thought it signified approval.

Cousin Myra had a talk with Father and Mother Osborne that night, and found them heartily in sympathy with her plans.

For the next week the Osbornes were agog with excitement and interest.

At first Cousin Myra made the suggestions, but their enthusiasm soon outstripped her, and they thought out things for themselves. Never did a week pass so quickly. And the Osbornes had never had such fun, either.

Christmas morning there was not a single present given or received at "The Firs" except those which Cousin Myra and Mr. and Mrs. Osborne gave to each other. The junior Osbornes had asked that the money which their parents had planned to spend in presents for them be given to them the previous week; and given it was, without a word.

The uncles and aunts arrived in due time, but not with them was the junior Osbornes' concern. They were the guests of Mr. and Mrs. Osborne. The junior Osbornes were having a Christmas dinner party of their own. In the small dining room a table was spread and loaded with good things. Ida and the twins cooked that dinner all by themselves. To be sure, Cousin Myra had helped some, and Frank and Darby had stoned all the raisins and helped pull the home-made candy; and all together they had decorated the small dining room royally with Christmas greens.

Then their guests came. First, all the little Rolands from the Hollow arrived--seven in all, with very red, shining faces and not a word to say for themselves, so shy were they. Then came a troop from French Joe's--four black-eyed lads, who never knew what shyness meant. Frank drove down to the village in the cutter and brought lame Sammy back with him, and soon after the last guest arrived--little Tillie Mather, who was Miss Rankin's "orphan 'sylum girl" from over the road.
Everybody knew that Miss Rankin never kept Christmas. She did not believe in it, she said, but she did not prevent Tillie from going to the Osbornes' dinner party.

Just at first the guests were a little stiff and unsocial; but they soon got acquainted, and so jolly was Cousin Myra--who had her dinner with the children in preference to the grown-ups--and so friendly the junior Osbornes, that all stiffness vanished. What a merry dinner it was! What peals of laughter went up, reaching to the big dining room across the hall, where the grown-ups sat in rather solemn state. And how those guests did eat and frankly enjoy the good things before them! How nicely they all behaved, even to the French Joes! Myra had secretly been a little dubious about those four mischievous-looking lads, but their manners were quite flawless. Mrs. French Joe had been drilling them for three days--ever since they had been invited to "de Chrismus dinner at de beeg house."

After the merry dinner was over, the junior Osbornes brought in a Christmas tree, loaded with presents. They had bought them with the money that Mr. and Mrs. Osborne had meant for their own presents, and a splendid assortment they were. All the French-Joe boys got a pair of skates apiece, and Sammy a set of beautiful books, and Tillie was made supremely happy with a big wax doll. Every little Roland got just what his or her small heart had been longing for. Besides, there were nuts and candies galore.

Then Frank hitched up his pony again, but this time into a great pung sleigh, and the junior Osbornes took their guests for a sleigh-drive, chaperoned by Cousin Myra. It was just dusk when they got back, having driven the Rolands and the French Joes and Sammy and Tillie to their respective homes.

"This has been the jolliest Christmas I ever spent," said Frank, emphatically.
"I thought we were just going to give the others a good time, but it was they who gave it to us," said Ida.

"Weren't the French Joes jolly?" giggled the twins. "Such cute speeches as they would make!"

"Me and Teddy Roland are going to be chums after this," announced Darby. "He's an inch taller than me, but I'm wider."

That night Frank and Ida and Cousin Myra had a little talk after the smaller Osbornes had been haled off to bed.

"We're not going to stop with Christmas, Cousin Myra," said Frank, at the end of it. "We're just going to keep on through the year. We've never had such a delightful old Christmas before."

"You've learned the secret of happiness," said Cousin Myra gently.

And the Osbornes understood what she meant.

Christmas at Red Butte

"Of course Santa Claus will come," said Jimmy Martin confidently.
Jimmy was ten, and at ten it is easy to be confident. "Why, he's _got_ to come because it is Christmas Eve, and he always _has_ come. You know that, twins."

Yes, the twins knew it and, cheered by Jimmy's superior wisdom, their doubts passed away. There had been one terrible moment when Theodora had sighed and told them they mustn't be too much disappointed if Santa Claus did not come this year because the crops had been poor, and he mightn't have had enough presents to go around.

"That doesn't make any difference to Santa Claus," scoffed Jimmy. "You know as well as I do, Theodora Prentice, that Santa Claus is rich whether the crops fail or not. They failed three years ago, before Father died, but Santa Claus came all the same. Prob'bly you don't remember it, twins, 'cause you were too little, but I do. Of course he'll come, so don't you worry a mite. And he'll bring my skates and your dolls. He knows we're expecting them, Theodora, 'cause we wrote him a letter last week, and threw it up the chimney. And there'll be candy and nuts, of course, and Mother's gone to town to buy a turkey. I tell you we're going to have a ripping Christmas."

"Well, don't use such slangy words about it, Jimmy-boy," sighed Theodora. She couldn't bear to dampen their hopes any further, and perhaps Aunt Elizabeth might manage it if the colt sold well. But

Theodora had her painful doubts, and she sighed again as she looked out of the window far down the trail that wound across the prairie, red-lighted by the declining sun of the short wintry afternoon.

"Do people always sigh like that when they get to be sixteen?" asked Jimmy curiously. "You didn't sigh like that when you were only fifteen, Theodora. I wish you wouldn't. It makes me feel funny—and it's not a nice kind of funniness either."

"It's a bad habit I've got into lately," said Theodora, trying to laugh. "Old folks are dull sometimes, you know, Jimmy-boy."

"Sixteen _is_ awful old, isn't it?" said Jimmy reflectively. "I'll tell you what _I'm_ going to do when I'm sixteen, Theodora. I'm going to pay off the mortgage, and buy mother a silk dress, and a piano for the twins. Won't that be elegant? I'll be able to do that 'cause I'm a man. Of course if I was only a girl I couldn't."

"I hope you'll be a good kind brave man and a real help to your mother," said Theodora softly, sitting down before the cosy fire and lifting the fat little twins into her lap.

"Oh, I'll be good to her, never you fear," assured Jimmy, squatting comfortably down on the little fur rug before the stove--the skin of the coyote his father had killed four years ago. "I believe in being good to your mother when you've only got the one. Now tell us a story, Theodora--a real jolly story, you know, with lots of fighting in it. Only please don't kill anybody. I like to hear about fighting, but I like to have all the people come out alive."

Theodora laughed, and began a story about the Riel Rebellion of '85—a story which had the double merit of being true and exciting at the same time. It was quite dark when she finished, and the twins were nodding, but Jimmy's eyes were wide open and sparkling.

"That was great," he said, drawing a long breath. "Tell us another."

"No, it's bedtime for you all," said Theodora firmly. "One story at a time is my rule, you know."

"But I want to sit up till Mother comes home," objected Jimmy.

"You can't. She may be very late, for she would have to wait to see Mr. Porter. Besides, you don't know what time Santa Claus might come--if he comes at all. If he were to drive along and see you children up instead of being sound asleep in bed, he might go right on and never call at all."

This argument was too much for Jimmy.

"All right, we'll go. But we have to hang up our stockings first. Twins, get yours."

The twins toddled off in great excitement, and brought back their Sunday stockings, which Jimmy proceeded to hang along the edge of the mantel shelf. This done, they all trooped obediently off to bed. Theodora gave another sigh, and seated herself at the window, where she could watch the moonlit prairie for Mrs. Martin's homecoming and knit at the same time.

I am afraid that you will think from all the sighing Theodora was doing that she was a very melancholy and despondent young lady. You couldn't think anything more unlike the real Theodora. She was the jolliest, bravest girl of sixteen in all Saskatchewan, as her shining brown eyes and rosy, dimpled cheeks would have told you; and her sighs were not on her own account, but simply for fear the children were going to be disappointed. She knew that they would be almost heartbroken if Santa Claus did not come, and that this would hurt the patient hardworking little mother more than all else.

Five years before this, Theodora had come to live with Uncle George and Aunt Elizabeth in the little log house at Red Butte. Her own mother had just died, and Theodora had only her big brother Donald left, and Donald had Klondike fever. The Martins were poor, but they had gladly made room for their little niece, and Theodora had lived there ever since, her aunt's right-hand girl and the beloved playmate of the children. They had been very happy until Uncle George's death two years before this Christmas Eve; but since then there had been hard times in the little log house, and though Mrs. Martin and Theodora did their best, it was a woefully hard task to make both ends meet, especially this year when their crops had been poor. Theodora and her aunt had made every sacrifice possible for the children's sake, and at least Jimmy and the twins had not felt the pinch very severely yet.

At seven Mrs. Martins bells jingled at the door and Theodora flew out. "Go right in and get warm, Auntie," she said briskly. "I'll take Ned away and unharness him."

"It's a bitterly cold night," said Mrs. Martin wearily. There was a note of discouragement in her voice that struck dismay to Theodora's heart.

"I'm afraid it means no Christmas for the children tomorrow," she thought sadly, as she led Ned away to the stable. When she returned to the kitchen Mrs. Martin was sitting by the fire, her face in her chilled hand, sobbing convulsively.

"Auntie--oh, Auntie, don't!" exclaimed Theodora impulsively. It was such a rare thing to see her plucky, resolute little aunt in tears. "You're cold and tired--I'll have a nice cup of tea for you in a trice."

"No, it isn't that," said Mrs. Martin brokenly "It was seeing those stockings hanging there. Theodora, I couldn't get a thing for the children--not a single thing. Mr. Porter would only give forty dollars for the colt, and when all the bills were paid there was barely enough left for such necessaries as we must have. I suppose I ought to feel thankful I could get those. But the thought of the children's disappointment tomorrow is more than I can bear. It would have been better to have told them long ago, but I kept building on getting more for the colt. Well, it's weak and foolish to give way like this. We'd better both take a cup of tea and go to bed. It will save fuel."

When Theodora went up to her little room her face was very thoughtful. She took a small box from her table and carried it to the window. In it was a very pretty little gold locket hung on a narrow blue ribbon. Theodora held it tenderly in her fingers, and looked out over the moonlit prairie with a very sober face. Could she give up her dear locket--the locket Donald had given her just before he started for the Klondike? She had never thought she could do such a thing. It was almost the only thing she had to remind her of Donald-- handsome, merry, impulsive, warmhearted Donald, who had gone away four years ago with a smile on his bonny face and splendid hope in his heart.

"Here's a locket for you, Gift o' God," he had said gaily--he had such a dear loving habit of calling her by the beautiful meaning of her name. A lump came into Theodora's throat as she remembered it. "I couldn't afford a chain too, but when I come back I'll bring you a rope of Klondike nuggets for it."

Then he had gone away. For two years letters had come from him regularly. Then he wrote that he had joined a prospecting party to a remote wilderness. After that was silence, deepening into anguish of suspense that finally ended in hopelessness. A rumour came that Donald Prentice was dead. None had returned from the expedition he had joined. Theodora had long ago given up all hope of ever seeing Donald again. Hence her locket was doubly dear to her.

But Aunt Elizabeth had always been so good and loving and kind to her. Could she not make the sacrifice for her sake? Yes, she could and would. Theodora flung up her head with a gesture that meant decision. She took out of the locket the bits of hair--her mother's and Donald's--which it contained (perhaps a tear or two fell as she did so) and then hastily donned her warmest cap and wraps. It was only three miles to Spencer; she could easily walk it in an hour and, as it was Christmas Eve, the shops would be open late. She muse walk, for Ned could not be taken out again, and the mare's foot was sore. Besides, Aunt Elizabeth must not know until it was done.

As stealthily as if she were bound on some nefarious errand, Theodora slipped downstairs and out of the house. The next minute she was hurrying along the trail in the moonlight. The great dazzling prairie was around her, the mystery and splendour of the northern night all about her. It was very calm and cold, but Theodora walked so briskly that she kept warm. The trail from Red Butte to Spencer was a lonely one. Mr. Lurgan's house, halfway to town, was the only dwelling on it.

When Theodora reached Spencer she made her way at once to the only jewellery store the little town contained. Mr. Benson, its owner, had been a friend of her uncle's, and Theodora felt sure that he would buy her locket. Nevertheless her heart beat quickly, and her breath came and went uncomfortably fast as she went in. Suppose he wouldn't buy it. Then there would be no Christmas for the children at Red
Butte.

"Good evening, Miss Theodora," said Mr. Benson briskly. "What can I do for you?"

"I'm afraid I'm not a very welcome sort of customer, Mr. Benson," said Theodora, with an uncertain smile. "I want to sell, not buy. Could you--will you buy this locket?"

Mr. Benson pursed up his lips, took up the locket, and examined it. "Well, I don't often buy second-hand stuff," he said, after some reflection, "but I don't mind obliging you, Miss Theodora. I'll give you four dollars for this trinket."

Theodora knew the locket had cost a great deal more than that, but four dollars would get what she wanted, and she dared not ask for more. In a few minutes the locket was in Mr. Benson's possession, and Theodora, with four crisp new bills in her purse, was hurrying to the toy store. Half an hour later she was on her way back to Red Butte, with as many parcels as she could carry--Jimmy's skates, two lovely dolls for the twins, packages of nuts and candy, and a nice plump turkey. Theodora beguiled her lonely tramp by picturing the children's joy in the morning.

About a quarter of a mile past Mr. Lurgan's house the trail curved suddenly about a bluff of poplars. As Theodora rounded the turn she halted in amazement. Almost at her feet the body of a man was lying across the road. He was clad in a big fur coat, and had a fur cap pulled well down over his forehead and ears. Almost all of him that could be seen was a full bushy beard. Theodora had no idea who he was, or where he had come from. But she realized that he was unconscious, and that he would speedily freeze to death if help were not brought. The footprints of a horse galloping across the prairie suggested a fall and a runaway, but Theodora did not waste time in speculation. She ran back at full speed to Mr. Lurgan's, and roused the household. In a few minutes Mr. Lurgan and his son had hitched a horse to a wood-sleigh, and hurried down the trail to the unfortunate man.

Theodora, knowing that her assistance was not needed, and that she ought to get home as quickly as possible, went on her way as soon as she had seen the stranger in safe keeping. When she reached the little log house she crept in, cautiously put the children's gifts in their stockings, placed the turkey on the table where Aunt Elizabeth would see it the first thing in the morning, and then slipped off to bed, a very weary but very happy girl.

The joy that reigned in the little log house the next day more than repaid Theodora for her sacrifice.

"Whoopee, didn't I tell you that Santa Claus would come all right!" shouted the delighted Jimmy. "Oh, what splendid skates!"

The twins hugged their dolls in silent rapture, but Aunt Elizabeth's face was the best of all.

Then the dinner had to be prepared, and everybody had a hand in that. Just as Theodora, after a grave peep into the oven, had announced that the turkey was done, a sleigh dashed around the house. Theodora flew to answer the knock at the door, and there stood Mr. Lurgan and a big, bewhiskered, fur-coated fellow whom Theodora recognized as the stranger she had found on the trail. But--_was_ he a stranger? There was something oddly familiar in those merry brown eyes. Theodora felt herself growing dizzy.

"Donald!" she gasped. "Oh, Donald!"

And then she was in the big fellow's arms, laughing and crying at the same time.

Donald it was indeed. And then followed half an hour during which everybody talked at once, and the turkey would have been burned to a crisp had it not been for the presence of mind of Mr. Lurgan who, being the least excited of them all, took it out of the oven, and set it on the back of the stove.

"To think that it was you last night, and that I never dreamed it," exclaimed Theodora. "Oh, Donald, if I hadn't gone to town!"

"I'd have frozen to death, I'm afraid," said Donald soberly. "I got into Spencer on the last train last night. I felt that I must come right out--I couldn't wait till morning. But there wasn't a team to be got for love or money--it was Christmas Eve and all the livery rigs were out. So I came on horseback. Just by that bluff something frightened my horse, and he shied violently. I was half asleep and thinking of my little sister, and I went off like a shot. I suppose I struck my head against a tree. Anyway, I knew nothing more until I came to in Mr. Lurgan's kitchen. I wasn't much hurt--feel none the worse of it except for a sore head and shoulder. But, oh, Gift o' God, how you have grown! I can't realize that you are the little sister I left four years ago. I suppose you have been thinking I was dead?"

"Yes, and, oh, Donald, where _have_ you been?"

"Well, I went way up north with a prospecting party. We had a tough time the first year, I can tell you, and some of us never came back. We weren't in a country where post offices were lying round loose either, you see. Then at last, just as we were about giving up in despair, we struck it rich. I've brought a snug little pile home with me, and things are going to look up in this log house, Gift o' God. There'll be no more worrying for you dear people over mortgages."

"I'm so glad--for Auntie's sake," said Theodora, with shining eyes. "But, oh, Donald, it's best of all just to have you back. I'm so perfectly happy that I don't know what to do or say."

"Well, I think you might have dinner," said Jimmy in an injured tone.
"The turkey's getting stone cold, and I'm most starving. I just can't stand it another minute."

So, with a laugh, they all sat down to the table and ate the merriest
Christmas dinner the little log house had ever known.

The Christmas Surprise at Enderly Road

"Phil, I'm getting fearfully hungry. When are we going to strike civilization?"

The speaker was my chum, Frank Ward. We were home from our academy for the Christmas holidays and had been amusing ourselves on this sunshiny December afternoon by a tramp through the "back lands," as the barrens that swept away south behind the village were called. They were grown over with scrub maple and spruce, and were quite pathless save for meandering sheep tracks that crossed and recrossed, but led apparently nowhere.

Frank and I did not know exactly where we were, but the back lands were not so extensive but that we would come out somewhere if we kept on. It was getting late and we wished to go home.

"I have an idea that we ought to strike civilization somewhere up the Enderly Road pretty soon," I answered.

"Do you call _that_ civilization?" said Frank, with a laugh.

No Blackburn Hill boy was ever known to miss an opportunity of flinging a slur at Enderly Road, even if no Enderly Roader were by to feel the sting.

Enderly Road was a miserable little settlement straggling back from Blackburn Hill. It was a forsaken looking place, and the people, as a rule, were poor and shiftless. Between Blackburn Hill and Enderly Road very little social intercourse existed and, as the Road people resented what they called the pride of Blackburn Hill, there was a good deal of bad feeling between the two districts.

Presently Frank and I came out on the Enderly Road. We sat on the fence a few minutes to rest and discuss our route home. "If we go by the road it's three miles," said Frank. "Isn't there a short cut?"

"There ought to be one by the wood-lane that comes out by Jacob Hart's," I answered, "but I don't know where to strike it."

"Here is someone coming now; we'll inquire," said Frank, looking up the curve of the hard-frozen road. The "someone" was a little girl of about ten years old, who was trotting along with a basketful of school books on her arm. She was a pale, pinched little thing, and her jacket and red hood seemed very old and thin.

"Hello, missy," I said, as she came up, and then I stopped, for I saw she had been crying.

"What is the matter?" asked Frank, who was much more at ease with children than I was, and had always a warm spot in his heart for their small troubles. "Has your teacher kept you in for being naughty?"

The mite dashed her little red knuckles across her eyes and answered indignantly, "No, indeed. I stayed after school with Minnie Lawler to sweep the floor."

"And did you and Minnie quarrel, and is that why you are crying?" asked Frank solemnly.

"Minnie and I _never_ quarrel. I am crying because we can't have the school decorated on Monday for the examination, after all. The Dickeys have gone back on us ... after promising, too," and the tears began to swell up in the blue eyes again.

"Very bad behaviour on the part of the Dickeys," commented Frank. "But can't you decorate the school without them?"

"Why, of course not. They are the only big boys in the school. They said they would cut the boughs, and bring a ladder tomorrow and help us nail the wreaths up, and now they won't ... and everything is spoiled ... and Miss Davis will be so disappointed."

By dint of questioning Frank soon found out the whole story. The semi-annual public examination was to be held on Monday afternoon, the day before Christmas. Miss Davis had been drilling her little flock for the occasion; and a program of recitations, speeches, and dialogues had been prepared. Our small informant, whose name was Maggie Bates, together with Minnie Lawler and several other little girls, had conceived the idea that it would be a fine thing to decorate the schoolroom with greens. For this it was necessary to ask the help of the boys. Boys were scarce at Enderly school, but the Dickeys, three in number, had promised to see that the thing was done.

"And now they won't," sobbed Maggie. "Matt Dickey is mad at Miss Davis 'cause she stood him on the floor today for not learning his lesson, and he says he won't do a thing nor let any of the other boys help us.
Matt just makes all the boys do as he says. I feel dreadful bad, and so does Minnie."

"Well, I wouldn't cry any more about it," said Frank consolingly. "Crying won't do any good, you know. Can you tell us where to find the wood-lane that cuts across to Blackburn Hill?" Maggie could, and gave us minute directions. So, having thanked her, we left her to pursue her disconsolate way and betook ourselves homeward.

"I would like to spoil Matt Dickey's little game," said Frank. "He is evidently trying to run things at Enderly Road school and revenge himself on the teacher. Let us put a spoke in his wheel and do Maggie a good turn as well."

"Agreed. But how?"

Frank had a plan ready to hand and, when we reached home, we took his sisters, Carrie and Mabel, into our confidence; and the four of us worked to such good purpose all the next day, which was Saturday, that by night everything was in readiness.

At dusk Frank and I set out for the Enderly Road, carrying a basket, a small step-ladder, an unlit lantern, a hammer, and a box of tacks. It was dark when we reached the Enderly Road schoolhouse. Fortunately, it was quite out of sight of any inhabited spot, being surrounded by woods. Hence, mysterious lights in it at strange hours would not be likely to attract attention.

The door was locked, but we easily got in by a window, lighted our lantern, and went to work. The schoolroom was small, and the old-fashioned furniture bore marks of hard usage; but everything was very snug, and the carefully swept floor and dusted desks bore testimony to the neatness of our small friend Maggie and her chum Minnie.

Our basket was full of mottoes made from letters cut out of cardboard and covered with lissome sprays of fir. They were, moreover, adorned with gorgeous pink and red tissue roses, which Carrie and Mabel had contributed. We had considerable trouble in getting them tacked up properly, but when we had succeeded, and had furthermore surmounted doors, windows, and blackboard with wreaths of green, the little Enderly Road schoolroom was quite transformed.

"It looks nice," said Frank in a tone of satisfaction. "Hope Maggie will like it."

We swept up the litter we had made, and then scrambled out of the window.

"I'd like to see Matt Dickey's face when he comes Monday morning," I laughed, as we struck into the back lands.

"I'd like to see that midget of a Maggie's," said Frank. "See here, Phil, let's attend the examination Monday afternoon. I'd like to see our decorations in daylight."

We decided to do so, and also thought of something else. Snow fell all day Sunday, so that, on Monday morning, sleighs had to be brought out. Frank and I drove down to the store and invested a considerable share of our spare cash in a varied assortment of knick-knacks. After dinner we drove through to the Enderly Road schoolhouse, tied our horse in a quiet spot, and went in. Our arrival created quite a sensation for, as a rule, Blackburn Hillites did not patronize Enderly Road functions. Miss Davis, the pale, tired-looking little teacher, was evidently pleased, and we were given seats of honour next to the minister on the platform.

Our decorations really looked very well, and were further enhanced by two large red geraniums in full bloom which, it appeared, Maggie had brought from home to adorn the teacher's desk. The side benches were lined with Enderly Road parents, and all the pupils were in their best attire. Our friend Maggie was there, of course, and she smiled and nodded towards the wreaths when she caught our eyes.

The examination was a decided success, and the program which followed was very creditable indeed. Maggie and Minnie, in particular, covered themselves with glory, both in class and on the platform. At its close, while the minister was making his speech, Frank slipped out; when the minister sat down the door opened and Santa Claus himself, with big fur coat, ruddy mask, and long white beard, strode into the room with a huge basket on his arm, amid a chorus of surprised "Ohs" from old and young.

Wonderful things came out of that basket. There was some little present for every child there--tops, knives, and whistles for the boys, dolls and ribbons for the girls, and a "prize" box of candy for everybody, all of which Santa Claus presented with appropriate remarks. It was an exciting time, and it would have been hard to decide which were the most pleased, parents, pupils, or teacher.

In the confusion Santa Claus discreetly disappeared, and school was dismissed. Frank, having tucked his toggery away in the sleigh, was waiting for us outside, and we were promptly pounced upon by Maggie and Minnie, whose long braids were already adorned with the pink silk ribbons which had been their gifts.

"_You_ decorated the school," cried Maggie excitedly. "I know you did.

I told Minnie it was you the minute I saw it."

"You're dreaming, child," said Frank.

"Oh, no, I'm not," retorted Maggie shrewdly, "and wasn't Matt Dickey mad this morning! Oh, it was such fun. I think you are two real nice boys and so does Minnie--don't you Minnie?"

Minnie nodded gravely. Evidently Maggie did the talking in their partnership.

"This has been a splendid examination," said Maggie, drawing a long breath. "Real Christmassy, you know. We never had such a good time before."

"Well, it has paid, don't you think?" asked Frank, as we drove home.

"Rather," I answered.

It did "pay" in other ways than the mere pleasure of it. There was always a better feeling between the Roaders and the Hillites thereafter. The big brothers of the little girls, to whom our Christmas surprise had been such a treat, thought it worthwhile to bury the hatchet, and quarrels between the two villages became things of the past.

Uncle Richard's New Year's Dinner
(1910)

Prissy Baker was in Oscar Miller's store New Year's morning, buying matches--for New Year's was not kept as a business holiday in Quincy--when her uncle, Richard Baker, came in. He did not look at Prissy, nor did she wish him a happy New Year; she would not have dared. Uncle Richard had not been on speaking terms with her or her father, his only brother, for eight years.

He was a big, ruddy, prosperous-looking man--an uncle to be proud of, Prissy thought wistfully, if only he were like other people's uncles, or, indeed, like what he used to be himself. He was the only uncle Prissy had, and when she had been a little girl they had been great friends; but that was before the quarrel, in which Prissy had had no share, to be sure, although Uncle Richard seemed to include her in his rancour.

Richard Baker, so he informed Mr. Miller, was on his way to Navarre with a load of pork.

"I didn't intend going over until the afternoon," he said, "but Joe Hemming sent word yesterday he wouldn't be buying pork after twelve today. So I have to tote my hogs over at once. I don't care about doing business New Year's morning."

"Should think New Year's would be pretty much the same as any other day to you," said Mr. Miller, for Richard Baker was a bachelor, with only old Mrs. Janeway to keep house for him.

"Well, I always like a good dinner on New Year's," said Richard Baker.

"It's about the only way I can celebrate. Mrs. Janeway wanted to spend the day with her son's family over at Oriental, so I was laying out to cook my own dinner. I got everything ready in the pantry last night, 'fore I got word about the pork. I won't get back from Navarre before one o'clock, so I reckon I'll have to put up with a cold bite."

After her Uncle Richard had driven away, Prissy walked thoughtfully home. She had planned to spend a nice, lazy holiday with the new book her father had given her at Christmas and a box of candy. She did not even mean to cook a dinner, for her father had had to go to town that morning to meet a friend and would be gone the whole day. There was nobody else to cook dinner for. Prissy's mother had died when Prissy was a baby. She was her father's housekeeper, and they had jolly times together.

But as she walked home, she could not help thinking about Uncle Richard. He would certainly have cold New Year cheer, enough to chill the whole coming year. She felt sorry for him, picturing him returning from Navarre, cold and hungry, to find a fireless house and an uncooked dinner in the pantry.

Suddenly an idea popped into Prissy's head. Dared she? Oh, she never could! But he would never know--there would be plenty of time—she would!

Prissy hurried home, put her matches away, took a regretful peep at her unopened book, then locked the door and started up the road to Uncle Richard's house half a mile away. She meant to go and cook Uncle Richard's dinner for him, get it all beautifully ready, then slip away before he came home. He would never suspect her of it. Prissy would not have him suspect for the world; she thought he would be more likely to throw a dinner of her cooking out of doors than to eat it.

Eight years before this, when Prissy had been nine years old, Richard and Irving Baker had quarrelled over the division of a piece of property. The fault had been mainly on Richard's side, and that very fact made him all the more unrelenting and stubborn. He had never spoken to his brother since, and he declared he never would. Prissy and her father felt very badly over it, but Uncle Richard did not seem to feel badly at all. To all appearance he had completely forgotten that there were such people in the world as his brother Irving and his niece Prissy.

Prissy had no trouble in breaking into Uncle Richard's house, for the woodshed door was unfastened. She tripped into the hostile kitchen with rosy cheeks and mischief sparkling in her eyes. This was an adventure--this was fun! She would tell her father all about it when he came home at night and what a laugh they would have!

There was still a good fire in the stove, and in the pantry Prissy found the dinner in its raw state--a fine roast of fresh pork, potatoes, cabbage, turnips and the ingredients of a raisin pudding, for Richard Baker was fond of raisin puddings, and could make them as well as Mrs. Janeway could, if that was anything to boast of.

In a short time the kitchen was full of bubbling and hissings and appetizing odours. Prissy enjoyed herself hugely, and the raisin pudding, which she rather doubtfully mixed up, behaved itself beautifully.

"Uncle Richard said he'd be home by one," said Prissy to herself, as the clock struck twelve, "so I'll set the table now, dish up the dinner, and leave it where it will keep warm until he gets here. Then I'll slip away home. I'd like to see his face when he steps in. I suppose he'll think one of the Jenner girls across the street has cooked his dinner."

Prissy soon had the table set, and she was just peppering the turnips when a gruff voice behind her said:

"Well, well, what does this mean?"

Prissy whirled around as if she had been shot, and there stood Uncle
Richard in the woodshed door!

Poor Prissy! She could not have looked or felt more guilty if Uncle Richard had caught her robbing his desk. She did not drop the turnips for a wonder; but she was too confused to set them down, so she stood there holding them, her face crimson, her heart thumping, and a horrible choking in her throat.

"I--I--came up to cook your dinner for you, Uncle Richard," she stammered. "I heard you say--in the store--that Mrs. Janeway had gone home and that you had nobody to cook your New Year's dinner for you. So I thought I'd come and do it, but I meant to slip away before you came home."

Poor Prissy felt that she would never get to the end of her explanation. Would Uncle Richard be angry? Would he order her from the house?

"It was very kind of you," said Uncle Richard drily. "It's a wonder your father let you come."

"Father was not home, but I am sure he would not have prevented me if he had been. Father has no hard feelings against you, Uncle Richard."

"Humph!" said Uncle Richard. "Well, since you've cooked the dinner you must stop and help me eat it. It smells good, I must say. Mrs. Janeway always burns pork when she roasts it. Sit down, Prissy. I'm hungry."

They sat down. Prissy felt quite giddy and breathless, and could hardly eat for excitement; but Uncle Richard had evidently brought home a good appetite from Navarre, and he did full justice to his New Year's dinner. He talked to Prissy too, quite kindly and politely, and when the meal was over he said slowly:

"I'm much obliged to you, Prissy, and I don't mind owning to you that I'm sorry for my share in the quarrel, and have wanted for a long time to be friends with your father again, but I was too ashamed and proud to make the first advance. You can tell him so for me, if you like. And if he's willing to let bygones be bygones, tell him I'd like him to come up here with you tonight when he gets home and spend the evening with me."

"Oh, he will come, I know!" cried Prissy joyfully. "He has felt so badly about not being friendly with you, Uncle Richard. I'm as glad as can be."

Prissy ran impulsively around the table and kissed Uncle Richard. He looked up at his tall, girlish niece with a smile of pleasure.

"You're a good girl, Prissy, and a kind-hearted one too, or you'd never have come up here to cook a dinner for a crabbed old uncle who deserved to eat cold dinners for his stubbornness. It made me cross today when folks wished me a happy New Year. It seemed like mockery when I hadn't a soul belonging to me to make it happy. But it has brought me happiness already, and I believe it will be a happy year all the way through."

"Indeed it will!" laughed Prissy. "I'm so happy now I could sing. I believe it was an inspiration--my idea of coming up here to cook your dinner for you."

"You must promise to come and cook my New Year's dinner for me every New Year we live near enough together," said Uncle Richard.

And Prissy promised.

Matthew Insists on Puffed Sleeves

Matthew was having a bad ten minutes of it. He had come into the kitchen, in the twilight of a cold, grey December evening, and had sat down in the wood-box corner to take off his heavy boots, unconscious of the fact that Anne and a bevy of her schoolmates were having a practice of "The Fairy Queen" in the sitting-room. Presently they came trooping through the hall and out into the kitchen, laughing and chattering gaily. They did not see Matthew, who shrank bashfully back into the shadows beyond the wood-box with a boot in one hand and a bootjack in the other, and he watched them shyly for the aforesaid ten minutes as they put on caps and jackets and talked about the dialogue and the concert. Anne stood among them, bright eyed and animated as they; but Matthew suddenly became conscious that there was something about her different from her mates. And what worried Matthew was that the difference impressed him as being something that should not exist.

Anne had a brighter face, and bigger, starrier eyes, and more delicate features than the others; even shy, unobservant Matthew had learned to take note of these things; but the difference that disturbed him did not consist in any of these respects. Then in what did it consist?

Matthew was haunted by this question long after the girls had gone, arm in arm, down the long, hard-frozen lane and Anne had betaken herself to her books. He could not refer it to Marilla, who, he felt, would be quite sure to sniff scornfully and remark that the only difference she saw between Anne and the other girls was that they sometimes kept their tongues quiet while Anne never did. This, Matthew felt, would be no great help.

He had recourse to his pipe that evening to help him study it out, much to Marilla's disgust. After two hours of smoking and hard reflection Matthew arrived at a solution of his problem. Anne was not dressed like the other girls!

The more Matthew thought about the matter the more he was convinced that Anne never had been dressed like the other girls--never since she had come to Green Gables. Marilla kept her clothed in plain, dark dresses, all made after the same unvarying pattern. If Matthew knew there was such a thing as fashion in dress it is as much as he did; but he was quite sure that Anne's sleeves did not look at all like the sleeves the other girls wore. He recalled the cluster of little girls he had seen around her that evening--all gay in waists of red and blue and pink and white--and he wondered why Marilla always kept her so plainly and soberly gowned.

Of course, it must be all right. Marilla knew best and Marilla was bringing her up. Probably some wise, inscrutable motive was to be served thereby. But surely it would do no harm to let the child have one pretty dress--something like Diana Barry always wore. Matthew decided that he would give her one; that surely could not be objected to as an unwarranted putting in of his oar. Christmas was only a fortnight off. A nice new dress would be the very thing for a present. Matthew, with a sigh of satisfaction, put away his pipe and went to bed, while Marilla opened all the doors and aired the house.

The very next evening Matthew betook himself to Carmody to buy the dress, determined to get the worst over and have done with it. It would be, he felt assured, no trifling ordeal. There were some things Matthew could buy and prove himself no mean bargainer; but he knew he would be at the mercy of shopkeepers when it came to buying a girl's dress.

After much cogitation Matthew resolved to go to Samuel Lawson's store instead of William Blair's. To be sure, the Cuthberts always had gone to William Blair's; it was almost as much a matter of conscience with them as to attend the Presbyterian church and vote Conservative. But William Blair's two daughters frequently waited on customers there and Matthew held them in absolute dread. He could contrive to deal with them when he knew exactly what he wanted and could point it out; but in such a matter as this, requiring explanation and consultation, Matthew felt that he must be sure of a man behind the counter. So he would go to Lawson's, where Samuel or his son would wait on him.

Alas! Matthew did not know that Samuel, in the recent expansion of his business, had set up a lady clerk also; she was a niece of his wife's and a very dashing young person indeed, with a huge, drooping pompadour, big, rolling brown eyes, and a most extensive and bewildering smile. She was dressed with exceeding smartness and wore several bangle bracelets that glittered and rattled and tinkled with every movement of her hands. Matthew was covered with confusion at finding her there at all; and those bangles completely wrecked his wits at one fell swoop.

"What can I do for you this evening. Mr. Cuthbert?" Miss Lucilla Harris inquired, briskly and ingratiatingly, tapping the counter with both hands.

"Have you any--any--any--well now, say any garden rakes?" stammered
Matthew.

Miss Harris looked somewhat surprised, as well she might, to hear a man inquiring for garden rakes in the middle of December.

"I believe we have one or two left over," she said, "but they're upstairs in the lumber-room. I'll go and see."

During her absence Matthew collected his scattered senses for another effort.

When Miss Harris returned with the rake and cheerfully inquired: "Anything else tonight, Mr. Cuthbert?" Matthew took his courage in both hands and replied: "Well now, since you suggest it, I might as well--take--that is--look at--buy some--some hayseed."

Miss Harris had heard Matthew Cuthbert called odd. She now concluded that he was entirely crazy.

"We only keep hayseed in the spring," she explained loftily. "We've none on hand just now."

"Oh, certainly--certainly--just as you say," stammered unhappy Matthew, seizing the rake and making for the door. At the threshold he recollected that he had not paid for it and he turned miserably back. While Miss Harris was counting out his change he rallied his powers for a final desperate attempt.

"Well now--if it isn't too much trouble--I might as well--that is--I'd like to look at--at--some sugar."

"White or brown?" queried Miss Harris patiently.

"Oh--well now--brown," said Matthew feebly.

"There's a barrel of it over there," said Miss Harris, shaking her bangles at it. "It's the only kind we have."

"I'll--I'll take twenty pounds of it," said Matthew, with beads of perspiration standing on his forehead.

Matthew had driven halfway home before he was his own man again. It had been a gruesome experience, but it served him right, he thought, for committing the heresy of going to a strange store. When he reached home he hid the rake in the tool-house, but the sugar he carried in to Marilla.

"Brown sugar!" exclaimed Marilla. "Whatever possessed you to get so much? You know I never use it except for the hired man's porridge or black fruit-cake. Jerry's gone and I've made my cake long ago. It's not good sugar, either--it's coarse and dark--William Blair doesn't usually keep sugar like that."

"I--I thought it might come in handy sometime," said Matthew, making good his escape.

When Matthew came to think the matter over he decided that a woman was required to cope with the situation. Marilla was out of the question. Matthew felt sure she would throw cold water on his project at once. Remained only Mrs. Lynde; for of no other woman in Avonlea would Matthew have dared to ask advice. To Mrs. Lynde he went accordingly, and that good lady promptly took the matter out of the harassed man's hands.

"Pick out a dress for you to give Anne? To be sure I will. I'm going to Carmody tomorrow and I'll attend to it. Have you something particular in mind? No? Well, I'll just go by my own judgment then. I believe a nice rich brown would just suit Anne, and William Blair has some new gloria in that's real pretty. Perhaps you'd like me to make it up for her, too, seeing that if Marilla was to make it Anne would probably get wind of it before the time and spoil the surprise? Well, I'll do it. No, it isn't a mite of trouble. I like sewing. I'll make it to fit my niece, Jenny Gillis, for she and Anne are as like as two peas as far as figure goes."

"Well now, I'm much obliged," said Matthew, "and--and--I dunno—but I'd like--I think they make the sleeves different nowadays to what they used to be. If it wouldn't be asking too much I--I'd like them made in the new way."

"Puffs? Of course. You needn't worry a speck more about it, Matthew. I'll make it up in the very latest fashion," said Mrs. Lynde. To herself she added when Matthew had gone: "It'll be a real satisfaction to see that poor child wearing something decent for once. The way Marilla dresses her is positively ridiculous, that's what, and I've ached to tell her so plainly a dozen times. I've held my tongue though, for I can see Marilla doesn't want advice and she thinks she knows more about bringing children up than I do for all she's an old maid. But that's always the way. Folks that has brought up children know that there's no hard and fast method in the world that'll suit every child. But them as never have think it's all as plain and easy as Rule of Three--just set your three terms down so fashion, and the sum'll work out correct. But flesh and blood don't come under the head of arithmetic and that's where Marilla Cuthbert makes her mistake. I suppose she's trying to cultivate a spirit of humility in Anne by dressing her as she does: but it's more likely to cultivate envy and discontent. I'm sure the child must feel the difference between her clothes and the other girls'. But to think of Matthew taking notice of it! That man is waking up after being asleep for over sixty years."

Marilla knew all the following fortnight that Matthew had something on his mind, but what it was she could not guess, until Christmas Eve, when Mrs. Lynde brought up the new dress. Marilla behaved pretty well on the whole, although it is very likely she distrusted Mrs. Lynde's diplomatic explanation that she had made the dress because Matthew was afraid Anne would find out about it too soon if Marilla made it.

"So this is what Matthew has been looking so mysterious over and grinning about to himself for two weeks, is it?" she said a little stiffly but tolerantly. "I knew he was up to some foolishness. Well, I must say I don't think Anne needed any more dresses. I made her three good, warm, serviceable ones this fall, and anything more is sheer extravagance. There's enough material in those sleeves alone to make a waist, I declare there is. You'll just pamper Anne's vanity, Matthew, and she's as vain as a peacock now. Well, I hope she'll be satisfied at last, for I know she's been hankering after those silly sleeves ever since they came in, although she never said a word after the first. The puffs have been getting bigger and more ridiculous right along; they're as big as balloons now. Next year anybody who wears them will have to go through a door sideways."

Christmas morning broke on a beautiful white world. It had been a very mild December and people had looked forward to a green Christmas; but just enough snow fell softly in the night to transfigure Avonlea. Anne peeped out from her frosted gable window with delighted eyes. The firs in the Haunted Wood were all feathery and wonderful; the birches and wild cherry trees were outlined in pearl; the ploughed fields were stretches of snowy dimples; and there was a crisp tang in the air that was glorious. Anne ran downstairs singing until her voice re-echoed through Green Gables.

"Merry Christmas, Marilla! Merry Christmas, Matthew! Isn't it a lovely Christmas? I'm so glad it's white. Any other kind of Christmas doesn't seem real, does it? I don't like green Christmases. They're _not_ green--they're just nasty faded browns and greys. What makes people call them green? Why--why--Matthew, is that for me? Oh, Matthew!"

Matthew had sheepishly unfolded the dress from its paper swathings and held it out with a deprecatory glance at Marilla, who feigned to be contemptuously filling the teapot, but nevertheless watched the scene out of the corner of her eye with a rather interested air.

Anne took the dress and looked at it in reverent silence. Oh, how pretty it was--a lovely soft brown gloria with all the gloss of silk; a skirt with dainty frills and shirrings; a waist elaborately in-tucked in the most fashionable way, with a little ruffle of filmy lace at the neck. But the sleeves--they were the crowning glory! Long elbow cuffs, and above them two beautiful puffs divided by rows of shirring and bows of brown silk ribbon.

"That's a Christmas present for you, Anne," said Matthew shyly.

"Why--why--Anne, don't you like it? Well now--well now."

For Anne's eyes had suddenly filled with tears.

"_Like_ it! Oh, Matthew!" Anne laid the dress over a chair and clasped her hands. "Matthew, it's perfectly exquisite. Oh, I can never thank you enough. Look at those sleeves! Oh, it seems to me this must be a happy dream."

"Well, well, let us have breakfast," interrupted Marilla. "I must say, Anne, I don't think you needed the dress; but since Matthew has got it for you, see that you take good care of it. There's a hair ribbon Mrs. Lynde left for you. It's brown, to match the dress. Come now, sit in."

"I don't see how I'm going to eat breakfast," said Anne rapturously. "Breakfast seems so commonplace at such an exciting moment. I'd rather feast my eyes on that dress. I'm so glad that puffed sleeves are still fashionable. It did seem to me that I'd never get over it if they went out before I had a dress with them. I'd never have felt quite satisfied, you see. It was lovely of Mrs. Lynde to give me the ribbon, too. I feel that I ought to be a very good girl indeed. It's at times like this I'm sorry I'm not a model little girl; and I always resolve that I will be in future. But somehow it's hard to carry out your resolutions when irresistible temptations come. Still, I really will make an extra effort after this."

When the commonplace breakfast was over Diana appeared, crossing the white log bridge in the hollow, a gay little figure in her crimson ulster. Anne flew down the slope to meet her.

"Merry Christmas, Diana! And oh, it's a wonderful Christmas. I've something splendid to show you. Matthew has given me the loveliest dress, with _such_ sleeves. I couldn't even imagine any nicer."

"I've got something more for you," said Diana breathlessly. "Here--this box. Aunt Josephine sent us out a big box with ever so many things in it--and this is for you. I'd have brought it over last night, but it didn't come until after dark, and I never feel very comfortable coming through the Haunted Wood in the dark now."

Anne opened the box and peeped in. First a card with "For the Anne-girl and Merry Christmas," written on it; and then, a pair of the daintiest little kid slippers, with beaded toes and satin bows and glistening buckles.

"Oh," said Anne, "Diana, this is too much, I must be dreaming."

"_I_ call it providential," said Diana. "You won't have to borrow Ruby's slippers now, and that's a blessing, for they're two sizes too big for you, and it would be awful to hear a fairy shuffling. Josie Pye would be delighted. Mind you, Rob Wright went home with Gertie Pye from the practice night before last. Did you ever hear anything equal to that?"

All the Avonlea scholars were in a fever of excitement that day, for the hall had to be decorated and a last grand rehearsal held.

The concert came off in the evening and was a pronounced success. The little hall was crowded; all the performers did excellently well, but Anne was the bright particular star of the occasion, as even envy, in the shape of Josie Pye, dared not deny.

"Oh, hasn't it been a brilliant evening?" sighed Anne, when it was all over and she and Diana were walking home together under a dark, starry sky.

"Everything went off very well," said Diana practically. "I guess we must have made as much as ten dollars. Mind you, Mr. Allan is going to send an account of it to the Charlottetown papers."

"Oh, Diana, will we really see our names in print? It makes me thrill to think of it. Your solo was perfectly elegant, Diana. I felt prouder than you did when it was encored. I just said to myself, 'It is my dear bosom friend who is so honoured.'"

"Well, your recitations just brought down the house, Anne. That sad one was simply splendid."

"Oh, I was so nervous, Diana. When Mr. Allan called out my name I really cannot tell how I ever got up on that platform. I felt as if a million eyes were looking at me and through me, and for one dreadful moment I was sure I couldn't begin at all. Then I thought of my lovely puffed sleeves and took courage. I knew that I must live up to those sleeves, Diana. So I started in, and my voice seemed to be coming from ever so far away. I just felt like a parrot. It's providential that I practised those recitations so often up in the garret, or I'd never have been able to get through. Did I groan all right?"

"Yes, indeed, you groaned lovely," assured Diana.

"I saw old Mrs. Sloane wiping away tears when I sat down. It was splendid to think I had touched somebody's heart. It's so romantic to take part in a concert isn't it? Oh, it's been a very memorable occasion indeed."

"Wasn't the boys' dialogue fine?" said Diana. "Gilbert Blythe was just splendid. Anne, I do think it's awful mean the way you treat Gil. Wait till I tell you. When you ran off the platform after the fairy dialogue one of your roses fell out of your hair. I saw Gil pick it up and put it in his breast pocket. There now. You're so romantic that I'm sure you ought to be pleased at that."

"It's nothing to me what that person does," said Anne loftily. "I simply never waste a thought on him, Diana."

That night Marilla and Matthew, who had been out to a concert for the first time in twenty years, sat for awhile by the kitchen fire after Anne had gone to bed.

"Well now, I guess our Anne did as well as any of them," said Matthew proudly.

"Yes, she did," admitted Marilla. "She's a bright child, Matthew. And she looked real nice, too. I've been kind of opposed to this concert scheme, but I suppose there's no real harm in it after all. Anyhow, I was proud of Anne tonight, although I'm not going to tell her so."

"Well now, I was proud of her and I did tell her so 'fore she went upstairs," said Matthew. "We must see what we can do for her some of these days, Marilla. I guess she'll need something more than Avonlea school by and by."

"There's time enough to think of that," said Marilla. "She's only thirteen in March. Though tonight it struck me she was growing quite a big girl. Mrs. Lynde made that dress a mite too long, and it makes Anne look so tall. She's quick to learn and I guess the best thing we can do for her will be to send her to Queen's after a spell. But nothing need be said about that for a year or two yet."

"Well now, it'll do no harm to be thinking it over off and on," said Matthew. "Things like that are all the better for lots of thinking over."

The Red Room

You would have me tell you the story, Grandchild? 'Tis a sad one and best forgotten--few remember it now. There are always sad and dark stories in old families such as ours.

Yet I have promised and must keep my word. So sit down here at my feet and rest your bright head on my lap, that I may not see in your young eyes the shadows my story will bring across their bonny blue.

I was a mere child when it all happened, yet I remember it but too well, and I can recall how pleased I was when my father's stepmother, Mrs. Montressor--she not liking to be called grandmother, seeing she was but turned of fifty and a handsome woman still--wrote to my mother that she must send little Beatrice up to Montressor Place for the Christmas holidays. So I went joyfully though my mother grieved to part with me; she had little to love save me, my father, Conrad Montressor, having been lost at sea when but three months wed.

My aunts were wont to tell me how much I resembled him, being, so they said, a Montressor to the backbone; and this I took to mean commendation, for the Montressors were a well-descended and well-thought-of family, and the women were noted for their beauty. This I could well believe, since of all my aunts there was not one but was counted a pretty woman. Therefore I took heart of grace when I thought of my dark face and spindling shape, hoping that when I should be grown up I might be counted not unworthy of my race.

The Place was an old-fashioned, mysterious house, such as I delighted in, and Mrs. Montressor was ever kind to me, albeit a little stern, for she was a proud woman and cared but little for children, having none of her own.

But there were books there to pore over without let or hindrance—for nobody questioned of my whereabouts if I but kept out of the way—and strange, dim family portraits on the walls to gaze upon, until I knew each proud old face well, and had visioned a history for it in my own mind--for I was given to dreaming and was older and wiser than my years, having no childish companions to keep me still a child.

There were always some of my aunts at the Place to kiss and make much of me for my father's sake--for he had been their favourite brother. My aunts--there were eight of them--had all married well, so said people who knew, and lived not far away, coming home often to take tea with Mrs. Montressor, who had always gotten on well with her step-daughters, or to help prepare for some festivity or other—for they were notable housekeepers, every one.

They were all at Montressor Place for Christmas, and I got more petting than I deserved, albeit they looked after me somewhat more strictly than did Mrs. Montressor, and saw to it that I did not read too many fairy tales or sit up later at nights than became my years.

But it was not for fairy tales and sugarplums nor yet for petting that I rejoiced to be at the Place at that time. Though I spoke not of it to anyone, I had a great longing to see my Uncle Hugh's wife, concerning whom I had heard much, both good and bad.

My Uncle Hugh, albeit the oldest of the family, had never married until now, and all the countryside rang with talk of his young wife. I did not hear as much as I wished, for the gossips took heed to my presence when I drew anear and turned to other matters. Yet, being somewhat keener of comprehension than they knew, I heard and understood not a little of their talk. And so I came to know that neither proud Mrs. Montressor nor my good aunts, nor even my gentle mother, looked with overmuch favour on what my Uncle Hugh had done. And I did hear that Mrs. Montressor had chosen a wife for her stepson, of good family and some beauty, but that my Uncle Hugh would have none of her--a thing Mrs. Montressor found hard to pardon, yet might so have done had not my uncle, on his last voyage to the Indies--for he went often in his own vessels--married and brought home a foreign bride, of whom no one knew aught save that her beauty was a thing to dazzle the day and that she was of some strange alien blood such as ran not in the blue veins of the Montressors.

Some had much to say of her pride and insolence, and wondered if Mrs. Montressor would tamely yield her mistress-ship to the stranger. But others, who were taken with her loveliness and grace, said that the tales told were born of envy and malice, and that Alicia Montressor was well worthy of her name and station.

So I halted between two opinions and thought to judge for myself, but when I went to the Place my Uncle Hugh and his bride were gone for a time, and I had even to swallow my disappointment and bide their return with all my small patience.

But my aunts and their stepmother talked much of Alicia, and they spoke slightingly of her, saying that she was but a light woman and that no good would come of my Uncle Hugh's having wed her, with other things of a like nature. Also they spoke of the company she gathered around her, thinking her to have strange and unbecoming companions for a Montressor. All this I heard and pondered much over, although my good aunts supposed that such a chit as I would take no heed to their whisperings.

When I was not with them, helping to whip eggs and stone raisins, and being watched to see that I ate not more than one out of five, I was surely to be found in the wing hall, poring over my book and grieving that I was no more allowed to go into the Red Room.

The wing hall was a narrow one and dim, connecting the main rooms of the Place with an older wing, built in a curious way. The hall was lighted by small, square-paned windows, and at its end a little flight of steps led up to the Red Room.

Whenever I had been at the Place before--and this was often--I had passed much of my time in this same Red Room. It was Mrs. Montressor's sitting-room then, where she wrote her letters and examined household accounts, and sometimes had an old gossip in to tea. The room was low-ceilinged and dim, hung with red damask, and with odd, square windows high up under the eaves and a dark wainscoting all around it. And there I loved to sit quietly on the red sofa and read my fairy tales, or talk dreamily to the swallows fluttering crazily against the tiny panes.

When I had gone this Christmas to the Place I soon bethought myself of the Red Room--for I had a great love for it. But I had got no further than the steps when Mrs. Montressor came sweeping down the hall in haste and, catching me by the arm, pulled me back as roughly as if it had been Bluebeard's chamber itself into which I was venturing.

Then, seeing my face, which I doubt not was startled enough, she seemed to repent of her haste and patted me gently on the head.

"There, there, little Beatrice! Did I frighten you, child? Forgive an old woman's thoughtlessness. But be not too ready to go where you are not bidden, and never venture foot in the Red Room now, for it belongs to your Uncle Hugh's wife, and let me tell you she is not over fond of intruders."

I felt sorry overmuch to hear this, nor could I see why my new aunt should care if I went in once in a while, as had been my habit, to talk to the swallows and misplace nothing. But Mrs. Montressor saw to it that I obeyed her, and I went no more to the Red Room, but busied myself with other matters.

For there were great doings at the Place and much coming and going. My aunts were never idle; there was to be much festivity Christmas week and a ball on Christmas Eve. And my aunts had promised me--though not till I had wearied them of my coaxing--that I should stay up that night and see as much of the gaiety as was good for me. So I did their errands and went early to bed every night without complaint--though I did this the more readily for that, when they thought me safely asleep, they would come in and talk around my bedroom fire, saying that of Alicia which I should not have heard.

At last came the day when my Uncle Hugh and his wife were expected home--though not until my scanty patience was well nigh wearied out--and we were all assembled to meet them in the great hall, where a ruddy firelight was gleaming.

My Aunt Frances had dressed me in my best white frock and my crimson sash, with much lamenting over my skinny neck and arms, and bade me behave prettily, as became my bringing up. So I slipped in a corner, my hands and feet cold with excitement, for I think every drop of blood in my body had gone to my head, and my heart beat so hardly that it even pained me.

Then the door opened and Alicia--for so I was used to hearing her called, nor did I ever think of her as my aunt in my own mind—came in, and a little in the rear my tall, dark uncle.

She came proudly forward to the fire and stood there superbly while she loosened her cloak, nor did she see me at all at first, but nodded, a little disdainfully, it seemed, to Mrs. Montressor and my aunts, who were grouped about the drawing-room door, very ladylike and quiet.

But I neither saw nor heard aught at the time save her only, for her beauty, when she came forth from her crimson cloak and hood, was something so wonderful that I forgot my manners and stared at her as one fascinated--as indeed I was, for never had I seen such loveliness and hardly dreamed it.

Pretty women I had seen in plenty, for my aunts and my mother were counted fair, but my uncle's wife was as little like to them as a sunset glow to pale moonshine or a crimson rose to white day-lilies.

Nor can I paint her to you in words as I saw her then, with the long tongues of firelight licking her white neck and wavering over the rich masses of her red-gold hair.

She was tall--so tall that my aunts looked but insignificant beside her, and they were of no mean height, as became their race; yet no queen could have carried herself more royally, and all the passion and fire of her foreign nature burned in her splendid eyes, that might have been dark or light for aught that I could ever tell, but which seemed always like pools of warm flame, now tender, now fierce.

Her skin was like a delicate white rose leaf, and when she spoke I told my foolish self that never had I heard music before; nor do I ever again think to hear a voice so sweet, so liquid, as that which rippled over her ripe lips.

I had often in my own mind pictured this, my first meeting with Alicia, now in one way, now in another, but never had I dreamed of her speaking to me at all, so that it came to me as a great surprise when she turned and, holding out her lovely hands, said very graciously:
"And is this the little Beatrice? I have heard much of you--come, kiss me, child."

And I went, despite my Aunt Elizabeth's black frown, for the glamour of her loveliness was upon me, and I no longer wondered that my Uncle Hugh should have loved her.

Very proud of her was he too; yet I felt, rather than saw--for I was sensitive and quick of perception, as old-young children ever are--that there was something other than pride and love in his face when he looked on her, and more in his manner than the fond lover—as it were, a sort of lurking mistrust.

Nor could I think, though to me the thought seemed as treason, that she loved her husband overmuch, for she seemed half condescending and half disdainful to him; yet one thought not of this in her presence, but only remembered it when she had gone.

When she went out it seemed to me that nothing was left, so I crept lonesomely away to the wing hall and sat down by a window to dream of her; and she filled my thoughts so fully that it was no surprise when I raised my eyes and saw her coming down the hall alone, her bright head shining against the dark old walls.

When she paused by me and asked me lightly of what I was dreaming, since I had such a sober face, I answered her truly that it was of her--whereat she laughed, as one not ill pleased, and said half mockingly:

"Waste not your thoughts so, little Beatrice. But come with me, child, if you will, for I have taken a strange fancy to your solemn eyes. Perchance the warmth of your young life may thaw out the ice that has frozen around my heart ever since I came among these cold Montressors."

And, though I understood not her meaning, I went, glad to see the Red Room once more. So she made me sit down and talk to her, which I did, for shyness was no failing of mine; and she asked me many questions, and some that I thought she should not have asked, but I could not answer them, so 'twere little harm.

After that I spent a part of every day with her in the Red Room. And my Uncle Hugh was there often, and he would kiss her and praise her loveliness, not heeding my presence-- for I was but a child.

Yet it ever seemed to me that she endured rather than welcomed his caresses, and at times the ever-burning flame in her eyes glowed so luridly that a chill dread would creep over me, and I would remember what my Aunt Elizabeth had said, she being a bitter-tongued woman, though kind at heart--that this strange creature would bring on us all some evil fortune yet.

Then would I strive to banish such thoughts and chide myself for doubting one so kind to me.

When Christmas Eve drew nigh my silly head was full of the ball day and night. But a grievous disappointment befell me, for I awakened that day very ill with a most severe cold; and though I bore me bravely, my aunts discovered it soon, when, despite my piteous pleadings, I was put to bed, where I cried bitterly and would not be comforted. For I thought I should not see the fine folk and, more than all, Alicia.

But that disappointment, at least, was spared me, for at night she came into my room, knowing of my longing--she was ever indulgent to my little wishes. And when I saw her I forgot my aching limbs and burning brow, and even the ball I was not to see, for never was mortal creature so lovely as she, standing there by my bed.

Her gown was of white, and there was nothing I could liken the stuff to save moonshine falling athwart a frosted pane, and out from it swelled her gleaming breast and arms, so bare that it seemed to me a shame to look upon them. Yet it could not be denied they were of wondrous beauty, white as polished marble.

And all about her snowy throat and rounded arms, and in the masses of her splendid hair, were sparkling, gleaming stones, with hearts of pure light, which I know now to have been diamonds, but knew not then, for never had I seen aught of their like.

And I gazed at her, drinking in her beauty until my soul was filled, as she stood like some goddess before her worshipper. I think she read my thought in my face and liked it--for she was a vain woman, and to such even the admiration of a child is sweet.

Then she leaned down to me until her splendid eyes looked straight into my dazzled ones.

"Tell me, little Beatrice--for they say the word of a child is to be believed--tell me, do you think me beautiful?"

I found my voice and told her truly that I thought her beautiful beyond my dreams of angels--as indeed she was. Whereat she smiled as one well pleased.

Then my Uncle Hugh came in, and though I thought that his face darkened as he looked on the naked splendour of her breast and arms, as if he liked not that the eyes of other men should gloat on it, yet he kissed her with all a lover's fond pride, while she looked at him half mockingly.

Then said he, "Sweet, will you grant me a favour?"

And she answered, "It may be that I will."

And he said, "Do not dance with that man tonight, Alicia. I mistrust him much."

His voice had more of a husband's command than a lover's entreaty. She looked at him with some scorn, but when she saw his face grow black--for the Montressors brooked scant disregard of their authority, as I had good reason to know-- she seemed to change, and a smile came to her lips, though her eyes glowed balefully.

Then she laid her arms about his neck and--though it seemed to me that she had as soon strangled as embraced him--her voice was wondrous sweet and caressing as she murmured in his ear.

He laughed and his brow cleared, though he said still sternly, "Do not try me too far, Alicia."

Then they went out, she a little in advance and very stately.

After that my aunts also came in, very beautifully and modestly dressed, but they seemed to me as nothing after Alicia. For I was caught in the snare of her beauty, and the longing to see her again so grew upon me that after a time I did an undutiful and disobedient thing.

I had been straitly charged to stay in bed, which I did not, but got up and put on a gown. For it was in my mind to go quietly down, if by chance I might again see Alicia, myself unseen.

But when I reached the great hall I heard steps approaching and, having a guilty conscience, I slipped aside into the blue parlour and hid me behind the curtains lest my aunts should see me.

Then Alicia came in, and with her a man whom I had never before seen. Yet I instantly bethought myself of a lean black snake, with a glittering and evil eye, which I had seen in Mrs. Montressor's garden two summers agone, and which was like to have bitten me. John, the gardener, had killed it, and I verily thought that if it had a soul, it must have gotten into this man.

Alicia sat down and he beside her, and when he had put his arms about her, he kissed her face and lips. Nor did she shrink from his embrace, but even smiled and leaned nearer to him with a little smooth motion, as they talked to each other in some strange, foreign tongue.

I was but a child and innocent, nor knew I aught of honour and dishonour. Yet it seemed to me that no man should kiss her save only my Uncle Hugh, and from that hour I mistrusted Alicia, though I understood not then what I afterwards did.

And as I watched them--not thinking of playing the spy--I saw her face grow suddenly cold, and she straightened herself up and pushed away her lover's arms.

Then I followed her guilty eyes to the door, where stood my Uncle Hugh, and all the pride and passion of the Montressors sat on his lowering brow. Yet he came forward quietly as Alicia and the snake drew apart and stood up.

At first he looked not at his guilty wife but at her lover, and smote him heavily in the face. Whereat he, being a coward at heart, as are all villains, turned white and slunk from the room with a muttered oath, nor was he stayed.

My uncle turned to Alicia, and very calmly and terribly he said, "From this hour you are no longer wife of mine!"

And there was that in his tone which told that his forgiveness and love should be hers nevermore.

Then he motioned her out and she went, like a proud queen, with her glorious head erect and no shame on her brow.

As for me, when they were gone I crept away, dazed and bewildered enough, and went back to my bed, having seen and heard more than I had a mind for, as disobedient people and eavesdroppers ever do.

But my Uncle Hugh kept his word, and Alicia was no more wife to him, save only in name. Yet of gossip or scandal there was none, for the pride of his race kept secret his dishonour, nor did he ever seem other than a courteous and respectful husband.

Nor did Mrs. Montressor and my aunts, though they wondered much among themselves, learn aught, for they dared question neither their brother nor Alicia, who carried herself as loftily as ever, and seemed to pine for neither lover nor husband. As for me, no one dreamed I knew aught of it, and I kept my own counsel as to what I had seen in the blue parlour on the night of the Christmas ball.

After the New Year I went home, but ere long Mrs. Montressor sent for me again, saying that the house was lonely without little Beatrice. So I went again and found all unchanged, though the Place was very quiet, and Alicia went out but little from the Red Room.

Of my Uncle Hugh I saw little, save when he went and came on the business of his estate, somewhat more gravely and silently than of yore, or brought to me books and sweetmeats from town.

But every day I was with Alicia in the Red Room, where she would talk to me, oftentimes wildly and strangely, but always kindly. And though I think Mrs. Montressor liked our intimacy none too well, she said no word, and I came and went as I listed with Alicia, though never quite liking her strange ways and the restless fire in her eyes.

Nor would I ever kiss her, after I had seen her lips pressed by the snake's, though she sometimes coaxed me, and grew pettish and vexed when I would not; but she guessed not my reason.

March came in that year like a lion, exceedingly hungry and fierce, and my Uncle Hugh had ridden away through the storm nor thought to be back for some days.

In the afternoon I was sitting in the wing hall, dreaming wondrous day-dreams, when Alicia called me to the Red Room. And as I went, I marvelled anew at her loveliness, for the blood was leaping in her face and her jewels were dim before the lustre of her eyes. Her hand, when she took mine, was burning hot, and her voice had a strange ring.

"Come, little Beatrice," she said, "come talk to me, for I know not what to do with my lone self today. Time hangs heavily in this gloomy house. I do verily think this Red Room has an evil influence over me. See if your childish prattle can drive away the ghosts that riot in these dark old corners--ghosts of a ruined and shamed life! Nay, shrink not--do I talk wildly? I mean not all I say--my brain seems on fire, little Beatrice. Come; it may be you know some grim old legend if this room--it must surely have one. Never was place fitter for a dark deed! Tush! never be so frightened, child--forget my vagaries. Tell me now and I will listen."

Whereat she cast herself lithely on the satin couch and turned her lovely face on me. So I gathered up my small wits and told her what I was not supposed to know--how that, generations agone, a Montressor had disgraced himself and his name, and that, when he came home to his mother, she had met him in that same Red Room and flung at him taunts and reproaches, forgetting whose breast had nourished him; and that he, frantic with shame and despair, turned his sword against his own heart and so died. But his mother went mad with her remorse, and was kept a prisoner in the Red Room until her death.

So lamely told I the tale, as I had heard my Aunt Elizabeth tell it, when she knew not I listened or understood. Alicia heard me through and said nothing, save that it was a tale worthy of the Montressors.

Whereat I bridled, for I too was a Montressor, and proud of it.

But she took my hand soothingly in hers and said, "Little Beatrice, if tomorrow or the next day they should tell you, those cold, proud women, that Alicia was unworthy of your love, tell me, would you believe them?"

And I, remembering what I had seen in the blue parlour, was silent--for I could not lie. So she flung my hand away with a bitter laugh, and picked lightly from the table anear a small dagger with a jewelled handle.

It seemed to me a cruel-looking toy and I said so--whereat she smiled and drew her white fingers down the thin, shining blade in a fashion that made me cold.

"Such a little blow with this," she said, "such a little blow--and the heart beats no longer, the weary brain rests, the lips and eyes smile never again! 'Twere a short path out of all difficulties, my Beatrice."

And I, understanding her not, yet shivering, begged her to cast it aside, which she did carelessly and, putting a hand under my chin, she turned up my face to hers.

"Little, grave-eyed Beatrice, tell me truly, would it grieve you much if you were never again to sit here with Alicia in this same Red Room?"

And I made answer earnestly that it would, glad that I could say so much truly. Then her face grew tender and she sighed deeply.

Presently she opened a quaint, inlaid box and took from it a shining gold chain of rare workmanship and exquisite design, and this she hung around my neck, nor would suffer me to thank her but laid her hand gently on my lips.

"Now go," she said. "But ere you leave me, little Beatrice, grant me but the one favour--it may be that I shall never ask another of you. Your people, I know--those cold Montressors--care little for me, but with all my faults, I have ever been kind to you. So, when the morrow's come, and they tell you that Alicia is as one worse than dead, think not of me with scorn only but grant me a little pity — for I was not always what I am now, and might never have become so had a little child like you been always anear me, to keep me pure and innocent. And I would have you but the once lay your arms about my neck and kiss me."

And I did so, wondering much at her manner--for it had in it a strange tenderness and some sort of hopeless longing. Then she gently put me from the room, and I sat musing by the hall window until night fell darkly--and a fearsome night it was, of storm and blackness. And I thought how well it was that my Uncle Hugh had not to return in such a tempest. Yet, ere the thought had grown cold, the door opened and he strode down the hall, his cloak drenched and wind-twisted, in one hand a whip, as though he had but then sprung from his horse, in the other what seemed like a crumpled letter.

Nor was the night blacker than his face, and he took no heed of me as I ran after him, thinking selfishly of the sweetmeats he had promised to bring me--but I thought no more of them when I got to the door of the Red Room.

Alicia stood by the table, hooded and cloaked as for a journey, but her hood had slipped back, and her face rose from it marble-white, save where her wrathful eyes burned out, with dread and guilt and hatred in their depths, while she had one arm raised as if to thrust him back.

As for my uncle, he stood before her and I saw not his face, but his voice was low and terrible, speaking words I understood not then, though long afterwards I came to know their meaning.

And he cast foul scorn at her that she should have thought to fly with her lover, and swore that naught should again thwart his vengeance, with other threats, wild and dreadful enough.

Yet she said no word until he had done, and then she spoke, but what she said I know not, save that it was full of hatred and defiance and wild accusation, such as a mad woman might have uttered.

And she defied him even then to stop her flight, though he told her to cross that threshold would mean her death; for he was a wronged and desperate man and thought of nothing save his own dishonour.

Then she made as if to pass him, but he caught her by her white wrist; she turned on him with fury, and I saw her right hand reach stealthily out over the table behind her, where lay the dagger.

"Let me go!" she hissed.

And he said, "I will not."

Then she turned herself about and struck at him with the dagger—and never saw I such a face as was hers at the moment.

He fell heavily, yet held her even in death, so that she had to wrench herself free, with a shriek that rings yet in my ears on a night when the wind wails over the rainy moors. She rushed past me unheeding, and fled down the hall like a hunted creature, and I heard the heavy door clang hollowly behind her.

As for me, I stood there looking at the dead man, for I could neither move nor speak and was like to have died of horror. And presently I knew nothing, nor did I come to my recollection for many a day, when I lay abed, sick of a fever and more like to die than live.

So that when at last I came out from the shadow of death, my Uncle Hugh had been long cold in his grave, and the hue and cry for his guilty wife was well nigh over, since naught had been seen or heard of her since she fled the country with her foreign lover.

When I came rightly to my remembrance, they questioned me as to what I had seen and heard in the Red Room. And I told them as best I could, though much aggrieved that to my questions they would answer nothing save to bid me to stay still and think not of the matter.

Then my mother, sorely vexed over my adventures--which in truth were but sorry ones for a child--took me home. Nor would she let me keep Alicia's chain, but made away with it, how I knew not and little cared, for the sight of it was loathsome to me.

It was many years ere I went again to Montressor Place, and I never saw the Red Room more, for Mrs. Montressor had the old wing torn down, deeming its sorrowful memories dark heritage enough for the next Montressor.

So, Grandchild, the sad tale is ended, and you will not see the Red Room when you go next month to Montressor Place. The swallows still build under the eaves, though--I know not if you will understand their speech as I did.

Manufactured by Amazon.ca
Bolton, ON

20998986R00062